"WHERE DID YOU LEARN TO DANCE?"

"In Aunt Silvie's kitchen," Ladden said, "but watch your toes, because I can't talk and count at the same time."

Jasmine laughed and leaned into him involuntarily. Without missing a beat, he took up the slack and reduced the distance between them. "You look very nice," she said, and meant it.

"You," he said quietly, "are breathtaking. Unfortunately, I can't stare and count at the same time either."

Relaxing further into him, she told herself she shouldn't be having such a good time, but she didn't want it to end. Had she found what she was looking for? Or was theirs simply a strong physical attraction, elevated by their odd circumstances and sudden proximity. The song faded to an end. Their bodies stilled, but they did not release each other.

Slowly, oh so slowly, Ladden lowered his head, his gaze riveted on her mouth. She had plenty of time to stop him with a movement or a protest, but Jasmine simply listened to her heart pound and wet her lips in preparation for his kiss.

With his mouth a whisper away from hers, he stopped, as if giving her a last chance to resist him, but she could not. . . .

WHAT ARE *LOVESWEPT* ROMANCES?

They are stories of true romance and touching emotion. We believe those two very important ingredients are constants in our highly sensual and very believable stories in the LOVE-SWEPT line. Our goal is to give you, the reader, stories of consistently high quality that may sometimes make you laugh, sometimes make you cry, but are always fresh and creative and contain many delightful surprises within their pages.

Most romance fans read an enormous number of books. Those they truly love, they keep. Others may be traded with friends and soon forgotten. We hope that each LOVESWEPT romance will be a treasure—a "keeper." We will always try to publish

LOVE STORIES YOU'LL NEVER FORGET
BY AUTHORS YOU'LL ALWAYS REMEMBER

The Editors

YOUR WISH
IS MY
COMMAND

STEPHANIE
BANCROFT

BANTAM BOOKS
NEW YORK · TORONTO · LONDON · SYDNEY · AUCKLAND

YOUR WISH IS MY COMMAND

A Bantam Book / January 1998

ISBN 0-553-44608-8

Published simultaneously in the United States and Canada

Bantam Books are published by Bantam Books, a division of Bantam Dou-
bleday Dell Publishing Group, Inc. Its trademark, consisting of the words
"Bantam Books" and the portrayal of a rooster, is Registered in U.S.
Patent and Trademark Office and in other countries. Marca Registrada.
Bantam Books, 1540 Broadway, New York, New York 10036.

PRINTED IN THE UNITED STATES OF AMERICA

OPM   10 9 8 7 6 5 4 3 2 1

For Chris, who made my wishes
come true

Dear Reader,

Ah, the underdog—stuff fairy tales are made of. Is there anything more satisfying than seeing a character with the odds stacked against him overcome seemingly insurmountable obstacles to achieve what he desires most in the world? Once upon a time, there was a poor, working man named Ladden who desired the love of Jasmine, a beautiful lady seen most often on the arm of the governor. Little did Ladden know that a day of scavenging for antiques would render him the magical means for gaining Jasmine's heart. But before he realizes it, he has used up two wishes that mire him and the object of his affection in a scandal of gigantic proportions! And if he ever gets out of the mess he's created, what will he do with his last wish?

I jumped at the opportunity to bring a fairy tale to life for Loveswept readers. I immersed myself in weaving a tale that combined love, magic, and a happy ending. *Your Wish Is My Command* came to me in a rush powerful enough to make *me* believe in magic—Ladden and Jasmine's story simply had to be told. I hope you are swept away by this humorous, heartwarming romp; if you are, tell a friend about the wonderful love stories you've discovered through Loveswept. And now, for all of you who still believe in fairy tales . . . enjoy!

Afterward, drop me a note and let me know how I'm doing: Stephanie Bancroft, P.O. Box 2395, Alpharetta, GA 30023.

Stephanie Bancroft

P.S. If you've ever wondered what happened to the people you knew in high school (you know, the ones *most* and *least* likely), watch for the launch of my new Loveswept series in the fall of '98, *Where Are They Now?*

ONE

"Naked," Jasmine Crowne announced as she stood at the door of the governor's bedroom.

Her assistant, April, dropped a handful of color strips, scattering them across the wood floor. "E-Excuse me?" the woman stammered as she dropped to her knees to collect the wayward slips of paper.

Jasmine bent to help her. "The room looks a bit naked, don't you think?"

April seemed hesitant to agree, and Jasmine smiled to herself as she realized her unfortunate word choice inside her boyfriend's boudoir. "Unfinished," she amended.

"You're the expert, Ms. Crowne," April said breathlessly, eager to please.

"This room definitely needs a rug," Jasmine asserted, then sat back on her heels. "But I've been all over Sacramento and nothing seems quite right."

"I thought that nice Mr. Sanderson was looking for a rug for you," April said.

Amused, Jasmine nodded. April always referred to antiques dealer Ladden Sanderson as "that nice Mr. Sanderson." "He is, but so far even Ladden has come up empty-handed."

Her assistant adopted a skeptical expression. "How hard could it be to find a *rug*?"

"That's what I thought at first." Jasmine shrugged. "I honestly can't remember having so much trouble locating a single item, but every carpet I've seen is either the wrong color, or the wrong size, or too fussy, or too trendy." She handed the strips she'd collected to April and rose. "I guess I'll know it when I see it."

"Kind of like Mr. Right," April said dreamily.

Jasmine laughed at the woman's romantic notions. "I suppose, although at the moment this rug seems even more elusive."

April stood awkwardly and pushed up her heavy glasses. "Easy for you to say, Ms. Crowne— you're dating the governor."

Resisting the urge to reveal that dating the busiest man in the state wasn't all it was cracked up to be, Jasmine relented with a smile. "Touché."

"That nice Mr. Sanderson will find a rug for you—he won't let you down."

Jasmine crossed her arms, barely suppressing a grin. "That nice Mr. Sanderson is holding a table for me. Perhaps I'll pay him a visit and see if he's found a magic carpet for me yet," she teased.

Ladden Sanderson wrinkled his nose, trying to prevent a burgeoning sneeze. He stumbled through the rear entrance of his antiques store, searching for a place to set down the box of junk before his lungs exploded. Dropping his load on a battered coffee table with a clatter, he yanked a handkerchief out of his back pocket and succumbed to a ferocious sneeze.

"Damn dust!" he complained, sniffling, then glanced around his shop with a wry smile. Dust was his life. Along with dirt, mud, mold, mildew, rust, rot, grease, gunk, and various other earmarks of aged whatnots. Which was why his hands were always a mess—alternately soiled from handling the pieces he gathered from estate sales, stained from restoring the better finds, then raw from scrubbing them. He peered into the crate of metal bric-a-brac and frowned. Probably junk, all of it, but the clever auctioneer had bundled the box with the rug Ladden had had his eye on, so, worthless or not, it was now his.

Ladden rolled his aching shoulders. Yesterday's scavenging had yielded him two beautiful—but heavy—iron beds, and today his body was complaining. He might have considered leaving the carpet in the truck until the afternoon, but he was so anxious to examine his purchase he trotted back outside. He paused only long enough to inhale the cool, fresh October air and rid his head of the pungent odor of which all antiques seemed to reek, then reached into the back of his rickety delivery truck and carefully, as if it were a sleeping woman, lifted the rolled carpet to his shoulder.

Adrenaline pumped through his chest as he curled his fingers in the long fringe. He'd foraged through hundreds of great rugs in his quest to be *the* antique resource for Sacramento designers. But this rug . . . he knew it was special the second he unrolled it this morning in Hanson's auction hall. And the only sensation that topped the high of knowing he'd made a fabulous find was the anticipation that Jasmine Crowne, one of the city's top interior designers, would appreciate his tenacity and grace him with one of her amazing smiles as she said, "I'll take it!"

Just the image of her big green eyes and wide, curving mouth warmed his cheeks. And that dark, straight ponytail she wore down her back drove him absolutely wild wondering how her hair would look spilling around her shoulders, sliding through his fingers . . .

Ladden snorted at his musings. "Dream on, man," he muttered to himself as he eased his awkward load through the extra-wide doorway. Not only did Jasmine Crowne have a boyfriend, but the man had more buildings named after him than Ladden had calluses. And when people addressed him, they called him "Mr. Governor, sir" instead of "hey, you in the hat."

Stepping past a row of cobwebby trunks, he settled the rug on the hardwood floor of his crowded storeroom, then pushed aside armoires, chairs, curios, and other odd pieces to clear a large space. Heart pounding, he reached into the front pocket of his jeans and withdrew a small knife to cut the binding cords. With a flick of his wrist, he unfurled the carpet, then jerked back in surprise as dozens—no, hundreds—of multicolored butterflies emerged from the folds. "What the . . . ?"

Dumbstruck, Ladden stared as the beautiful insects whirled and floated around him, their wings making tiny thrumming noises as they flew past his ears. Where had they come from? He quickly knelt and ran his fingers over the hand-tied pile to look for hidden cocoons and larvae he had missed during the inspection. His fingers tingled from the buildup of static electricity on the wool surface, but the only discovery within the pile was an unexpectedly small amount of dust and loose fibers.

Ladden frowned. Maybe the rug wasn't as old as he had first assumed. Although the Mughal designs appeared to predate the 1800s, the colors seemed brighter and newer here under his own lighting. Perhaps the carpet was simply a convincing reproduction. He searched the surface frantically. At the auction house, he had counted four holes the size of his fist that would have to be repaired by the rug weaver across town. Where were they now? Was it possible he had picked up the wrong rug? Although it seemed unlikely that two rugs so similar would be available at the same auction, he pulled a scrap of paper where he'd written the item number from his shirt pocket and compared it with the yellow tag on the rug. No mistake.

With growing confusion, he stood and walked through the bizarre blizzard of butterflies making their way toward the open doorway. Ladden stopped in front of the makeshift library he stored in a single glass-front bookcase, fingered the spine of several reference books, then withdrew a dog-eared volume on Oriental-design rugs. Thumbing through the colorful pictures, he compared the closely spaced lilies and asters on a field of raspberry red to photos in the book. A wide black and a narrow cream-colored border surrounded the dominant red center of the bed-sized rug, and both the short sides were adorned with thick fringe nearly eight inches in length.

Two pictures showed rugs with similar markings, both attributed approximately to the late 1700s, and—Ladden swallowed—both boasting an asking price approaching twenty thousand dollars. He glanced back at his receipt. Even if the carpet were a copy, he'd received quite a bargain for the four thousand dollars that had nauseated him at the time. But he had felt . . . *compelled* to buy the rug. His arm kept raising his bid paddle of its own volition until the red-faced auctioneer had yelled, "Sold!"

Remembering the holes he'd imagined, he scratched his head. "Ladden, my man," he muttered, "*you* need a vacation." Then he laughed. With the money he'd make from this carpet, he might actually take one. Jasmine was in the middle of renovating her boyfriend's not-so-humble living quarters at the governor's mansion and had asked him to keep an eye out for a rug for the master bedroom. If she liked it as much as he thought she would, he knew money would be no object. Still . . .

He ran his fingers over the rug in admiration and bit the inside of his cheek, his chest filling up with that rare wonder of having found something so special that it seemed worthy of keeping. Which was a dangerous habit in the antiques business— and a rule to which Ladden had made very few exceptions in the last fifteen years. Oh well, he would keep it for a few days at least. Satisfied, he secured the carpet in a wooden hanger and hoisted it high against the rear wall of the crowded room, then called and left a message with an old acquaintance who knew more than he about valuing rugs.

Shooing as many of the mysterious stray butterflies outside as possible, he carried the crate with the questionable contents into his showroom. Since Mondays were set aside for estate sales, yard sales, and tracking down special requests, Tuesdays were typically busy with regular customers coming in to check out the latest acquisitions. Which meant Jasmine would be in this afternoon. He would have to decide whether to tell her about the carpet or save the unveiling for another day.

As always, pride welled within him as he glanced over his small but impressive display room. The building was old but beautiful and structurally intact. He owned the two rooms that housed his business, and although he needed to expand, the glorious display windows and enviable location on Pacific Street kept him rooted to the spot. He had loved the storefront on sight, especially since the alley gave him great access to the storeroom and space to park his big, ugly truck. He'd gambled and bought the place, although he and his eclectic mix of retail neighbors couldn't have known that a few years later, a ramp would be built from the highway onto Pacific. Instantly, their exposure, traffic, and property values had skyrocketed. Which had proved to be a double-edged sword, since now the chance of expanding into the shops on either side of him was almost nil. Even if the owners decided to sell, he couldn't afford to buy.

High ceilings and wood floors were the perfect backdrop for his treasures, and floor-to-ceiling shelves lined the entire wall behind his antique mahogany counter, evoking images of an upscale general store.

Carrying a bucket of supplies outside, Ladden quickly swept the sidewalk in front of his door and,

just as he had for fifteen years, moved down to do
the same for Mrs. Pickney of Pickney's Vacuum
Cleaner Sales & Service. The lights in her shop
were low, telling him she had not yet arrived for
the day. A streak of mud from last night's rain
marred her window, so he wiped it clean, then realized the mud was probably a result of a clogged
gutter and retrieved his ladder to remove a handful
of debris.

After returning to his shop, Ladden noted he
still had a few minutes to spare before opening. He
turned his attention to the box he'd been rail-
roaded into buying, wrinkling his nose when he
pulled out a broken horse harness, a few worthless
hubcaps, and a badly rusted iron skillet. He knew
it—junk. Garbage. Trash. Not even worth the
trouble of hauling off. Next came a handful of odd
hinges and cabinet hardware, a few holey hand
saws, and a dented brass teapot blackened with tar-
nish.

He picked through the rest of the rubble, most
of which was either unidentifiable or deteriorated
beyond repair. From the entire lot, he set aside
four glass doorknobs, and, at the last moment, the
scarred pot, as his cleanup projects for the day to
tackle between customers.

Sitting neatly on his large palm, the pot had a
nice shape, although it appeared to have weathered
a good deal of adventure. The piece was old, but
he couldn't pinpoint the decade or even the cen-
tury. Other than the lid, the pot was seamless,

fashioned from a single piece of metal. The wide-throated spout narrowed along its upturned length, the opening so minuscule Ladden doubted its functionality. Most likely, it had graced some lady's parlor sideboard alongside other dishes that were meant to be seen and not used, then been relegated to a little girl's tea set where it had been bounced off a few too many hard surfaces.

He chuckled, turning it over in his hands. On the side, barely discernible, were faint etchings. Ladden squinted and rubbed his finger lightly over the surface . . . words, perhaps, but he couldn't be sure. One thing seemed certain, however—the lid was stuck, soldered into place by years of corrosion and disuse. Which might explain why it had been cast aside in the first place.

After turning the sign on his door to Open and choosing a moody jazz station on the radio, he gathered a can of metal cleaner and a polishing rag and settled onto his high leather seat behind the counter. Whistling under his breath, Ladden concentrated on the brass pot to avoid mental calculations of how long it would be before Jasmine walked through his door, ringing his literal and figurative bells, respectively.

To his surprise, after only a few minutes of elbow grease, the teapot showed vast improvement: underneath the goo was not brass, but beautiful, lustrous copper. Ladden pursed his lips, the names of at least two copper collectors coming to mind. It wouldn't bring a mint, but it would buy a nice steak-and-wine dinner for two, he decided. Jasmine. How had he managed to fall for a woman he'd never have in a million years, not in his wildest dreams?

His raw, sensitive fingers grazed the unknown etchings beneath the thin cloth and just as he lifted the pot for a better look, he felt the first earthquake tremor. The windows rattled and glass and crystal pieces whined shrilly, sliding and bumping against the shelves. Jumping to his feet, Ladden looked around wildly before realizing the mahogany counter was the safest place to be and diving to the floor behind it.

For nearly a minute, he lay on his stomach with his arms over his head, listening to his store and its contents pop, groan, shake, and topple around him, thinking that at any second, something large and penetrating would impale him to the wood floor. The sound of crashing glass rang against his eardrums. The faces of family and friends flashed through his mind and he prayed they were all safe. Cool air blasted in and the bell above his door clanged with abandon as the doors banged open. The quaking grew more furious and Ladden felt as if he were spinning round and round, held in place only by centrifugal force.

And then everything stopped.

He lay still for a few seconds, then lifted his head cautiously. A foul stench filled his nostrils and he wondered if the sewers had ruptured. He pulled himself to his feet and leaned on the counter, slowly scanning the scene before him. Mayhem. Nearly every piece of furniture lay on its side amid broken debris. Dust motes rained down from the ceiling, rapidly furnishing a fuzzy coating for the room's contents. Appalled, Ladden dropped his head into his hands and groaned.

In unison with someone else.

He jerked his head up and glanced around, then heard the groan again, this time below him and in front of the counter. Heart pounding, Ladden picked his way quickly through the mess to find an elderly man leaning against the wood counter, his sandaled feet stretched out in front of him. The man wore a black turban over his white hair and seemed to be drowning in the layers of ragged sheets wrapped around his thin body.

Homeless, Ladden decided instantly. He must have ducked inside when he felt the quake. Ladden reached forward and gently pulled the man to his feet, suddenly realizing his visitor was the source of the powerful stench. "Are you okay, mister?"

The man lifted his gaze to Ladden, his brown eyes wide. "Where . . . where am I?" His voice sounded rusty but richly accented, his dark skin hinted of Middle Eastern ancestry.

"There was an earthquake," Ladden said carefully. "This is my antiques store. Are you hurt?"

The old man shook his head and ran his hands slowly over his limbs. "I'm human," he whispered.

Ladden felt a pang of sympathy. "Sure you are,

buddy. You're just a little down on your luck is all. Is anything broken?"

After a few seconds of silence in which the man tried to take in his surroundings, he croaked, "Yes, the spell—the spell is broken."

Senile, Ladden surmised. "Sir, are you hurt?"

"N-no," the man said, offering Ladden a weak smile. "I've been set free."

"Everyone in California finds religion sooner or later," Ladden agreed wryly, looking the man over. He appeared to be all right, at least physically. Ladden reached into his back pocket for his wallet, and extended a ten-dollar bill. "Here you go, pal. Get yourself something to eat, okay?"

The man accepted the money, holding it in his long-fingernailed hands as if he'd never seen anything like it. "But you have given me my life."

Ladden waved off his gratitude. "My store was the one you just happened to be walking by, that's all."

"But what do you want?" the man asked, grasping Ladden's shirt in his bony fists.

"Hey," Ladden said crossly, trying to pull away. "No need to get defensive—I don't want anything from you."

The man refused to relinquish his hold. "Gold? Jewels? Power? Anything you want, simply wish for it, and I shall grant you three of your heart's desires."

Ladden covered the man's icy hands with his own and gently pried the knotted fingers loose.

"Look, mister, you need to get back on your medication. There's a shelter two blocks over on Hargrove. I'm sure they can help you, so move along, okay?"

The sounds of the street floated in, reminding Ladden the double doors stood open. He straightened his shirt, then gently guided the man toward the door, dreading the certain melee out in the street. But instead of smashed cars, sagging utility lines, and buckled sidewalks, Pacific Street lay as calm as a deep lake. Pedestrians strolled by, engrossed in reaching their destinations, unconcerned by the recent disturbance. Ladden glanced back to find the homeless man had slipped away. Remembering Mrs. Pickney, he hurried next door and burst into her shop.

Mrs. Pickney stood at her counter watching a black-and-white portable television and drinking a cup of coffee. She smiled broadly. "Oh, good morning, Ladden. Would you like some coffee?"

"The quake! Didn't you feel it?" he cried in amazement.

Setting down her coffee cup with a frown, she asked, "What quake? When?"

"Just now!" Ladden exclaimed.

"No," Mrs. Pickney said, shaking her head slowly. "I didn't feel a thing—it must have been a very minor tremor."

"My place is in a shambles," he said, glancing at her undisturbed glass cases and wall displays.

She squinted. "Are you sure, dear?"

"Yes!"

"There has to be an explanation—" she began, then glanced up as a customer walked in. She smiled at Ladden. "I'll be over in a few minutes."

"Sure thing, Mrs. Pickney," Ladden mumbled. He stopped the young man who had entered her shop. "Sir, did you feel an earthquake about five minutes ago?"

"No," the man said, his brow creased. "Did you?"

"Uh . . . no," Ladden said with a small laugh. "I . . . I guess not." He waved to his neighbor. "Forget it, Mrs. Pickney—I'll see you later."

Apprehension descended over him as he returned to the quiet sidewalk. He poked his head into a handful of retail stores neighboring his and asked the retailers if they'd felt any ground disturbances, but each responded with an emphatic no, including the upholstery shop on the other side of him. He had almost convinced himself it hadn't happened at all until he stepped back into the bedlam in his showroom.

How was it possible that, other than the homeless man, he was the only person who had felt the earthquake? The only business on the street that had suffered any damage? He sighed. Days—it would take him days to get things back in order. Ladden mentally ticked off the things he'd have to do: call a building inspector, call his insurance agent, file a claim . . . He yanked off his cap, then ran his fingers through his hair. And he'd have to close down for a while. No one could conduct business in this mess.

He suddenly noticed the copper teapot in the middle of the floor, and Ladden squatted to pick it up. The lid was missing, undoubtedly dislodged when he dropped it. The homeless man's rantings echoed in his mind, and Ladden smiled. Three wishes. If only life were that easy.

Turning his sign back to Closed, he stopped in mid-motion. Across the street, Jasmine Crowne alighted from her luxury sports sedan, flipped her dark ponytail over her shoulder, and began walking toward his war-torn store.

"Damn," he muttered, his mind racing for a sane explanation for the colossal mess. *You see, Jasmine, this morning I experienced my own personal earthquake* . . .

TWO

Jasmine reached into her purse and activated her cellular phone in case Trey called her for lunch. She sighed. Such a call did not seem likely, considering the frantic pace of his campaign as election day drew near. Jasmine stepped up onto the sidewalk and put her hand on the familiar gargoyle doorknob of one of her favorite shops, Ladden's Castle. Her heart thumped when she realized someone was standing on the other side of the glass door, but she smiled warmly when she recognized Ladden.

When the knob refused to yield beneath her hand, she glanced at her watch, noticing the Closed sign. "Am I too early?" she yelled. She needed a lift today and Ladden Sanderson never failed to boost her spirits. The man was always so optimistic, his unreserved laughter so cheering . . . usually. This morning, he wore a strange expression.

"No," he yelled, "you're not too early."

But when he made no motion to unlock the door, she laughed. "Am I too late?"

Through the glass, she noticed how his dark hair curled up around the edge of the dusty baseball cap he wore. He bit his lower lip and shook his head. "No, you're not too late."

Puzzled, Jasmine gave him a wry grin. "You got a girl in there?" Which wouldn't surprise her, she decided. Although she hadn't noticed a girlfriend hanging around on her frequent visits to his store, Ladden was attractive: tall, with dark eyes and a trim, workingman's physique.

Finally, he grinned, too. "No girl," he yelled, then slowly unlocked the door and swung it open.

"For a minute, I thought you were trying to get rid—" Stopping just inside the door, she gaped at the clutter. "What on earth happened?"

Remarkably calm, Ladden cleared his throat, offering a little shrug. "Spring cleaning?"

She frowned. "It's almost November."

He rubbed his big hands together. "Then I'm even more behind than I thought."

Jasmine jammed her hands against her hips. "Ladden, what's going on? Were you burglarized?"

"No—not exactly."

"Then what, exactly?"

"A quake?" His voice climbed in question, as if he weren't sure himself.

"An earthquake?" Jasmine gasped. "When?"

"Just before you arrived?" Again, he sounded uncertain.

Her exasperation escalated. "Well, was it a quake, or wasn't it?"

"Er, yeah, I think so."

She blinked. "Weren't you here?"

"Yeah."

"And did the earth suddenly start to move and things begin to fall?"

"Yeah."

She had always considered Ladden very bright, but now she was starting to wonder. "Did you get hit on the head?"

He laughed, swept off his hat, and ran his hands through his flattened hair. "No, but that would explain a lot of things, I guess. To be honest, I'm not sure what happened, but if it was a quake, this might not be the safest place for you to be right now."

"Funny," she said thoughtfully, "I was having coffee nearby and didn't feel a thing." Her gaze fell on the remnants of black pottery littering the floor a few feet away. She gasped in dismay and scooped up a large broken chunk. "Oh, the Mc-Coy punch bowl—I nearly bought it last week and now I could kick myself!"

"Aw, it could have been much worse," Ladden said, putting his usual cheerful spin on things, she noted. "I haven't been back to the storeroom," he added, picking his way toward the rear, righting small pieces of toppled furniture as he went. "But the table I'm holding for you was heavy, so it should be all right."

Jasmine followed Ladden. Her heart felt heavy for him. He worked hard and ran a reputable business, and this bit of misfortune didn't seem fair. She stopped when a pile of broken glass blocked her path, then glanced up in surprise when she felt Ladden's hand on her arm.

"Careful." His broad fingers felt warm and strong on her skin. She watched the muscles bunch in his tanned forearm as he assumed her weight to help her across, amazed at the thrill of awareness that barbed through her.

"Thanks," she murmured when he released her. Ladden inclined his head, his easy smile crinkling his dark eyes around the corners and lighting his smooth face. Despite the dust, his uniform of jeans and T-shirt seemed to fit him especially well today, emphasizing his muscular shoulders. Jasmine shook off the train of thought, telling herself it had been too long since she and Trey had spent a romantic evening together.

They entered the brightly lit storeroom and Jasmine was pleased to see that the damage looked minimal since the contents consisted mainly of larger, less fragile pieces. "Looks like the table is fine," Ladden announced.

But Jasmine was no longer listening. She was

entralled. She crawled over an old trunk, sneezed, then ran her hand over the short, nubby pile of the most beautiful carpet she had ever seen. Static electricity crackled, sending a tingle through her fingertips. Only then did she notice the butterflies. At least a dozen brilliantly colored specimens dotted the carpet, their bodies still, but their wings moving with the quiet regularity of intermittent windshield wiper blades. The entire scene was somewhat . . . magical. "Ladden," she said in wonder, "where did you get this rug?"

He turned, eyes wide, then glanced at the bare wall behind her before answering. "I found it at Hanson's this morning." He picked up a large wooden clip from the floor, frowning at its clasp. "I hung it up to air out. The quake must have knocked it down. He scared away a few butterflies with a sweeping motion, then he turned a smile her way. "I thought you might like it."

"Like it? I love it," she breathed. "It's Persian, isn't it?"

Ladden nodded, running the back of his hand across the fibers. "But I can't date it—its condition is too good to be as old as I first guessed."

Her heart pounded. "I want it."

She looked up and saw his lips pressed together. Finally he dropped his gaze. "It might not be for sale."

Jasmine laughed merrily. "Ladden, I've seen you take down light fixtures from this store and sell them."

He nodded, stroking his chin. "I don't even know what it's worth. One of my experts is stopping by later this week to take a look at it. I think it's quite a find, though."

Jasmine lovingly traced the outline of an intricately woven flowering plant. "The governor would pay handsomely for something so dear."

"I'm sure he would," Ladden agreed in a subdued tone.

"A perfect complement to a quilt the Turkan prince gave him," Jasmine continued, imagining how magnificent the carpet would look on the pale hardwood in his bedroom.

"And if he isn't reelected?" Ladden asked, careful to keep his voice neither supportive nor reproachful.

Jasmine winced, the discouraging results of this week's polls flashing in her mind. Influencing state policy was everything to Trey—his ambition was the quality she admired most about him. He hadn't been afraid to tackle unpopular issues during his first term, and he seemed likely to pay for it on election day, but she didn't like to think about how much losing would crush him—or how much it might affect their fledgling relationship. She conjured up a smile for Ladden. "The governor owns several homes."

He stuffed his hands in his pockets. "Actually," he said abruptly, "I was thinking the carpet would look nice in *my* private quarters."

"Oh." She straightened, flipping her ponytail

out of her way. Of course Ladden would have his own place. She simply hadn't given it much thought before now. They had never broached personal subjects, although for the past few months, her own life had been chronicled on a regular basis in the local newspapers. The state held its collective breath to see if California's most eligible bachelor would marry. And she had to admit the prospect of being the governor's wife held no small amount of appeal. She forced herself to turn her attention back to Ladden and found his compelling gaze already on her. "Do you live nearby?"

"I have a fixer-upper in Glenhayden."

Jasmine couldn't contain her surprise. "Glenhayden? I grew up—" she stopped, then added, "spending summers near there." She didn't make a habit of sharing the extent of her meager upbringing. More often, she stuck to the loose background she had fabricated with just enough fact to keep the reporters happy.

"It's a nice, older community," Ladden said. "Do you still visit?"

"N-no," she said, nodding at the rug. "Let me know when you decide on a price."

"*If* I decide on a price," Ladden corrected with a grin, shaking his finger at her.

She laughed, suddenly struck by the revelation that she enjoyed his company, his good-natured banter. "I fully intend to wear you down," she warned.

His smile slipped just a bit, and she saw something akin to desire flicker in his brown eyes. "I'm looking forward to it."

And suddenly, she felt something leap between them, a feeling that stole the moisture from her mouth. How many conversations had she shared with Ladden over the past three years? It seemed as if she had always known him. But at this moment, she felt as if she were seeing him for the first time. Sexual awareness enveloped them. Panic rose in Jasmine's chest, panic that Ladden felt something emanating from her that she couldn't possibly mean. Could she?

"I—I'd better be going," she said, unable to drag her gaze from his. Goose bumps skittered along her arms, raising fine hairs and sending a shiver down her spine. She stumbled backward, remembering the trunk behind her a second too late. When she landed and the wind whooshed from her lungs, Jasmine faintly wished her sixth grade gym teacher could have witnessed her perfect backward somersault.

Ladden was at her side immediately. "Are you all right?" he asked, his mouth set in a grim line. He clasped her hand and leaned over her, searching her face. In his mad scramble, he had lost his hat. With his dark hair curling haphazardly, he looked boyish and incredibly sexy. And Jasmine presumed she had hit her head rather hard because, for the duration of a heartbeat, she wanted Ladden to gather her in his arms and kiss her.

With her first breath of air, she laughed, half because she must have looked foolish, half because she couldn't believe what she was thinking.

His face relaxed and his laughter joined hers. "I give you a nine-point-seven for technique."

Still on her back, she smiled. "You're just glad I'm okay so I won't sue you."

He lifted his arms to indicate the clutter around them. "What you see is what you get—no riches here."

She wet her lips. A direct comparison between him and the governor? She wasn't sure. "Are you going to help me up?"

He hesitated, then a mischievous smile creased his face. "I was hoping you'd faint so I could give you mouth-to-mouth resuscitation." He leaned closer, bracing one hand next to her shoulder. "I'm certified."

Her ears hummed with the sudden silence. He, too, had been affected by their close contact. But she had more sense than to allow these fleeting desires to spin out of control. "Certif*iable*, perhaps," she said, extending her hand. He gently pulled her to her feet. For a second she felt light-headed, but she wasn't sure whether to attribute it to her tumble or to her full-body proximity to Ladden.

"Are you sure you feel okay?" he asked, wrapping his fingers around her upper arms.

"Yes," she lied, then glanced down at her dusty slacks. "A little worse for wear," she muttered, stepping back to brush off her clothing—and to escape his disorienting nearness. "I really do need to get going."

He unearthed his hat, then blazed a safer trail through the debris to the front of the store. "I hope the damage isn't as bad as it looks," Jasmine offered sympathetically.

Ladden shrugged his big shoulders. "I needed to do inventory anyway."

Her foot nudged something and Jasmine glanced down at a wonderful little copper pot. "How quaint," she said, retrieving it from the littered floor and dusting it off. "It's an oil lamp."

"Nice quality," Ladden said. "I was cleaning it up when the quake struck this morning."

"Well, at least you didn't have a store full of customers."

"Yeah," he agreed. "Although some skinny old homeless man wandered in, scared out of his wits."

"I can't remember ever leaving here without buying something," Jasmine said, turning the lamp over in her hands. The lid was missing, but the piece would look nice on her fireplace mantel. "I'll take this."

He looked surprised. "Fine—give me a few hours to find the lid and finish cleaning it. Can you stop by later this afternoon?"

Jasmine mentally reviewed her schedule. "I need to drop off some cushions at the upholstery

shop next door. I can come back around six or so."
She refused to acknowledge the voice that whispered in her head: of course she was *not* already
anticipating the return trip.

"Just bang on the door," Ladden said. "I'll be
the guy with the broom."

Jasmine laughed, hesitating with her hand on
the doorknob. Ladden's dusty face wore a sunny
expression that belied his situation, and suddenly,
she didn't want to leave. Staying to help him clean
up sounded more enjoyable than the buying trips
she had planned for the afternoon—and the revelation shook her. "Well," she said, alarmed at
the tremor in her voice, "I'll see you later, Ladden."

He nodded and ran his hand along the counter.
After an awkward pause, he offered her a small
wave. "Later, Jasmine."

Feeling unsettled, she wondered if he had
wanted to say something else. She slowly walked
back to her car, trying to make sense of what—if
anything—had just transpired between them. She
sat with her hands on the wheel for a full minute,
her mind racing. Hormones, she decided. Hormones, pure and simple. Ladden was a good-looking, attentive man who exuded a physicality
that was hard to ignore. She was a normal, red-blooded woman who hadn't seen much of her boyfriend lately. Hormones.

But as she pulled away from the curb, Jasmine

couldn't resist a glance at his storefront in her rearview mirror. She bit her lip, hard. She had known the man for three years. Why was she noticing these disturbing things about him this morning?

THREE

Ladden held his breath until Jasmine's car disappeared from view. Then he reached for the broom and danced a jig with his spindly partner around the littered floor, humming along with the jaunty song on the radio. He wasn't absolutely, positively certain, but he felt as if they had finally connected. He swept off his hat and held it over his heart as he dipped the broom low in a swoon, then drawled, "Was that a spark of interest I saw in your lovely green eyes, my dear?"

At the sound of a knock on the window, Ladden bolted upright and jammed his hat back on his head. Mrs. Pickney stood outside with her hand to her brow, smiling and waving. Tingling with embarrassment, he pretended to sweep violently as he made his way to the door.

"My windows look suspiciously clean," she said as she stepped inside, "so thank you—" She gasped, covering her mouth, rendered speechless by the unsightly mess of his showroom. Ladden abandoned the broom and guided her to a dusty chair.

"It's okay, Mrs. Pickney, the damage seems to be isolated here and no one was injured."

"I—I don't understand," she murmured. "I didn't feel a thing—how . . . why . . ." She raised moist eyes. "It doesn't seem fair."

He shrugged and squeezed her frail shoulders. "It was a freak tremor. Don't worry—my insurance is paid up." Scanning the crowded showroom, he added, "Besides, I needed to scale down my inventory, anyway. It was getting too cramped in here."

She glanced around and finally grinned. "This place *was* starting to look like a fire hazard."

"See?" he said. "A blessing in disguise. Now, hadn't you better see to your customers?"

"I'll close for the day and help you clean up."

He shook his head. "No need—I can't do much until I contact my insurance agent anyway."

The color had returned to her cheeks. "You're right, of course." She rose from her chair and walked to the door. "Ladden, why do bad things happen to good people?"

Feeling a burst of affection for the woman, Ladden said, "Don't waste a minute worrying about me. I'll be fine."

She angled her white head at him. "I can't

imagine why some smart young lady hasn't scooped you up by now."

He adopted a lovelorn expression and sighed. "I'm waiting for you to realize our age difference doesn't matter, Mrs. Pickney."

Laughing, she waved him off and walked out.

After he locked the door, Ladden groaned, scrubbing his face with his hands. Despite his forced cheer, the damage the quake had wrought only heaped more pressure on the business decisions he'd have to make soon. Should he interpret this incident as an omen, a sign to move to another location, one large enough to offer him room to expand?

He retrieved the broom and leaned on it, thinking it would take a miracle to resolve his business dilemma. "I wish Mrs. Pickney would simply retire and give me her space," he announced to the disorderly room. Then he laughed wryly and began sweeping. Wishing wouldn't get him anywhere.

After he swept up most of the glass, he unearthed his Rolodex and made the necessary phone calls. His insurance agent, Saul Tydwell, a friend of his uncle's who always wore the same bad brown suit, arrived within the hour bearing stale donuts in condolence and a Polaroid camera.

"If you weren't Ernie's nephew," Saul said, shaking his head between snapshots, "I'd never believe you. You must be sitting on some kind of fault line—and the underwriter is going to love that."

"Tell me my rates won't go up," Ladden said, knowing the answer even before the little man offered him a sympathetic look.

"I'll shop around for a better rate, son, but it doesn't look good."

Ladden dropped his head in his hands and visualized the money in his bank account dwindling like sand in the top of an hourglass. He spent much of the afternoon turning away customers with explanations that became more vague as the day wore on. The building inspector's visit and subsequent ruling that the building was structurally sound seemed like the bright spot of the day until Ladden reached the bottom of the report. The inspector had noted with an asterisk that considering the results of interviews with surrounding retailers, he doubted that an earthquake had actually occurred. Meanwhile, his agent had called the state seismology department.

"Filing a false claim will get you in a heap of trouble, son," Saul said sternly over the phone. "Come on, Ladden, don't try to pull the wool over my eyes with some fake quake—it's too damn easy to trace." Then the man's voice softened. "If you're in trouble, busting up your place isn't the way to handle it. I'm sure your uncle Ernie would float you a loan."

"I'm telling you, it was an earthquake," Ladden said through clenched teeth.

"Then why doesn't the seismology department

have a record of it, and why did no one else feel it?"

"I don't know," Ladden began. "Wait, there *was* someone else, a homeless man who wandered in from the street."

"Do you know this man?"

Ladden sighed in frustration. "No, and even if I could find him, he acted senile."

"I see," Saul said dubiously. "Well, I'm telling you, the claim will be denied if you insist on turning in this cockamamie story about an earthquake."

"Are you saying you want me to lie?" Ladden asked, his voice rising in anger.

"Look, son, you haven't filed a claim in fifteen years and you always pay your premiums on time. I'm trying to help you out. Think hard about what really happened and call me tomorrow."

Ladden listened to the dial tone for a few seconds, then raised the phone over his head, ready to fling it against the wall. But he stopped there—he couldn't afford to buy a new phone. He set the instrument gently on the table, then mouthed every curse word he'd ever heard, and made up a few of his own.

Glancing at his watch, his spirits lifted a notch. Jasmine would be back within an hour, and he had made progress in the cleanup. Of course, he noted in one of the few unbroken mirrors, he was now wearing most of the store's grime. He banged his hat on his leg, stirring up another dust cloud, then trudged back through the storeroom toward his shower. He'd promised to stop by the family tavern to help celebrate a cousin's birthday, so he needed to be presentable, he reasoned. Cleaning up didn't have anything to do with Jasmine coming back.

He showered quickly and pulled on the only spare clothes he had at the shop—worn jeans and a dark red flannel shirt that was missing a button, and low-heeled black boots. With his pocketknife, he dug dirt from beneath his fingernails until they stung, then scrubbed his knuckles raw with an old toothbrush. He needed a haircut, he concluded as he fought to tame the dark curls that seemed determined to flip up around his ears and collar. Rubbing his whisker-shadowed chin, he longed for a razor, but his makeshift toiletries bag was not so obliging. It did, however, furnish a travel-size bottle of musky cologne that had been popular a decade ago. He unscrewed the lid and took a whiff. Not bad, he decided, and splashed on a few drops. But, when he surveyed the results of his labor in the tarnished mirror, his shoulders dropped. Jasmine Crowne would never be interested in someone like him.

On his way back through the storeroom, he paused to admire the rug and scare the remaining butterflies toward an open window. Then he scratched his temple. He could have sworn he'd left the rug draped over those old trunks, and now it lay a few feet away, stretched smoothly across the massive table he was holding for Jasmine. Oh well, he'd moved everything in the store at least once today. It must have slipped his mind.

The front showroom looked brighter and shinier, although a little bare to his eyes. At least he'd found the lid to the copper lamp Jasmine had become so enamored of. He lifted the piece from the counter, impressed at how well it had turned out. Even the dents seemed less noticeable in the lustrous glow of the restored finish. The etchings on the side were in some kind of foreign language—probably the family's name, he mused. Or a recipe for disaster. He'd certainly had enough trouble since he brought the lamp home—and that rug. Then a thought struck him. Was it possible the copper lamp and the rug had come from the same household?

He grabbed a scrap of paper and copied the letters and symbols in case the woman who came to value the rug would find the information useful. He had just finished when he heard a knock on the door and glanced up to see Jasmine waving through the glass.

His heart thudded crazily as he unlocked the door. She, too, had changed from her dusty clothes and wore a loose, turquoise silk tunic over a slim, flowered skirt. The long, dark ponytail had been braided and hung over her left shoulder, clasped with a simple silver ring that matched the thick chain at her throat. Her bare legs were golden from a lingering tan and her own natural coloring, and she wore strappy sandals that exposed her pink toenails. She looked exotic, and Ladden didn't trust himself to speak.

"You made a lot of progress," she said, turning in place in front of the counter.

He nodded, his mind racing for something clever to say. "Yeah," he managed.

"Oh, and the lamp is beautiful!" she exclaimed, her eyes glowing as she lifted it and stroked the surface.

"Yeah." Why couldn't he think of something, anything, to say to prolong her stay?

"How much do I owe you?" she asked.

Ladden bit the inside of his cheek. He felt funny about charging her for a little whatnot, considering his heart was hers for the taking. "How about dinner?" he asked, as amazed at the words that came out of his mouth as Jasmine appeared to be.

"Dinner?" she asked, blinking her large green eyes.

"Sure." He leaned against the counter so he wouldn't fall down. "I know a great little place down the block with the best seafood in town."

The corners of her mouth turned up even as her brow furrowed. "That sounds nice, Ladden, but I don't think—"

Her response was cut short by the clanging bell on the door announcing another visitor. Ladden turned to see his Uncle Ernie lumbering inside, still dressed in his plumber's uniform of dark coveralls. "There you are, Lad. Your Aunt Silvie was getting worried about you, then I got a strange call from Saul a few minutes ago and thought I'd better see what's keeping you." The tall, burly man stopped and glanced at Jasmine with dancing eyes. "But I see what's keeping you."

"Er, Uncle Ernie," Ladden said with rising embarrassment, "this is Jasmine Crowne. Jasmine, Ernie Sanderson."

"Pleasure, little lady," Ernie said, offering her a big paw to shake.

"Same here," Jasmine said with a small smile.

"Well, come on," Ernie said, gesturing to Ladden. "Maddie is waiting to blow out the candles. Silvie will have one of her spells if that chocolate cake melts down."

Ladden shifted uncomfortably and jerked his head toward the door meaningfully. "You go ahead, Ernie, and tell them not to wait. I'll be there as soon as I can."

"That's all right," Jasmine interjected. "I need to be leaving, too."

"You're coming with Lad, aren't you?" Ernie asked, his bushy brows high on his creased forehead. "We have a family tavern and hangout. Ladden's Aunt Silvie would love to meet the woman in his life."

Ladden closed his eyes, tingling with humiliation. "Ernie, please go ahead."

"I really do need to go," Jasmine said hurriedly, tearing out a check and signing it quickly. "Let me know if this isn't enough," she said, stuffing the paper into Ladden's hand. She practically ran to the door, holding the copper lamp against her chest. Ladden's heart fell as she scrambled out the door.

"Thanks, Uncle Ernie," he said.

"What did I say?" Ernie demanded, throwing up his hands. "Are you sleeping with her?"

"No, I'm not sleeping with her! What's the matter with you?" Ladden bellowed.

"Ah," his uncle said, nodding calmly. He put his arm around Ladden's shoulder and steered him toward the door. "Then that explains why you're so aggravated."

"I'm starving," Ladden announced as he held open the door of Tabby's, the family watering hole for the last two decades, for his Uncle Ernie. He kissed his Aunt Silvie and pulled his young Cousin Maddie's ear after she blew out twelve of the thirteen candles on her chocolate cake, joining them in a booming rendition of "Happy Birthday." When the song was done, he crossed the spacious restaurant to the bar and yelled a greeting to Malone, the bartender.

"Here you go, Ladden," Malone said, sliding a mug of beer toward him.

Ladden pulled out his wallet, but Malone waved it off. "Drink up tonight, buddy," he said. "Your friend covered your tab."

Confused, Ladden asked, "What friend?"

Malone shrugged. "Some old guy with a turban. He gave me a brand-new hundred dollar bill and asked me to give you this note."

Frowning, Ladden took the small folded note and opened it. "A wise first wish, Master."

Jasmine walked briskly toward her car, more rattled now than she had been this morning. No one had asked her out since she'd started seeing Trey McDonald, and she liked the idea that everyone seemed to think she was off-limits—spoken for by one of the most powerful men in the state. No one had presumed to compete with his charm, his looks, his influence, his money . . . except Ladden Sanderson, a quiet, rough-around-the-edges man who, for the most part, made his living with his big hands and strong back.

What seemed even more incredible than his forwardness was her impulse to take him up on his offer. He had looked so appealing, standing there all scrubbed and brushed, his muscular body filling his clothes in the most sexy way. At the hopeful look in his dark eyes, she'd nearly buckled. The thrill she'd experienced at his invitation went beyond flattery. But she wasn't about to risk her current relationship over a strong physical attraction to a man who, although very nice, didn't share her lifelong goals, her circle of friends, or her ambition to rise as far as possible above the poverty she'd grown up in, in a shack on the outskirts of Glenhayden.

Jasmine squashed the unpleasant memories, then halted abruptly and looked around. "My car," she muttered. "I know I parked it right here." She craned her neck, looking up and down the street, pacing back and forth in front of the empty spot where she was sure she had left it. Panic bloomed in her chest—could it have been stolen?

"Are you looking for a white carriage?" a strange looking man wearing a turban yelled from across the street. He spoke with a rich accent and appeared to be selling watches from a card table.

Jasmine nodded. "Did you see it?"

"A big machine with a hook on the back pulled it away," he said matter-of-factly.

"Towed? Oh, no," Jasmine murmured, glancing at the expired parking meter she hadn't noticed before. She reached into her purse for her cell phone, then cursed when she saw the dark power light. Jasmine checked the time. Six-thirty—most shops were already closed for the evening, but she should be able to find a pay phone in a bar or restaurant. Morosely, she realized the press would have a field day when they discovered the governor's girlfriend's car had been towed because she hadn't paid a fifty-cent parking meter.

Your Wish Is My Command
41

She shouted at the watch man, "Can you tell me where I can find the nearest phone?"

The man screwed up his face in thought, then pointed in the direction she'd just come from. "That would be a place called Tabby's."

FOUR

Jasmine stepped gingerly into Tabby's, warming immediately to the cozy atmosphere. Buffed to a high sheen, the wood floor dipped and rolled from the passage of many feet over the years. An enormous pecan-colored bar lined the wall to her right, fronted by red upholstered stools, and aproned waitresses wound their way between tables surrounded by low, comfortable looking chairs, most of which were occupied in the height of the dinner hour. The din of conversation and laughter almost drowned out the background piano music. It was a nice, family place, Jasmine decided, seeing as many kids as adults enjoying the spaghetti and meatloaf.

The hostess greeted her just as she recognized Ladden standing at the bar, holding a beer in one hand and a piece of paper in the other. This must be his family's restaurant. With a jolt, she acknowledged a small thrill at seeing him again, even though seeing him in such a casual setting was a bit of a shock. How odd that she'd never really thought about Ladden's life outside of his shop. He was studying the paper with a creased brow, but when he glanced up and saw her, his dark eyes widened.

She raised her hand in a wave as he straightened and moved toward her. "Hi," she offered when he was within earshot.

"Hi," he said, his face wreathed in smiles. "I'm glad you changed your mind."

She twisted the bag that contained the copper lamp. Her palms felt suddenly damp. "Well, I didn't exactly. My car was towed and someone told me I could find a phone here."

One by one, his smiles dissolved. "Oh."

"This looks like a very nice place," she said hurriedly.

He shifted from one foot to the other, then inclined his head. "Thanks—I'll tell my cousins the governor's interior designer said so."

She knew he meant to pay her a compliment, but it didn't quite feel like one. And she wasn't sure why.

"Glad to see you changed your mind, little lady," boomed Ladden's Uncle Ernie as he stepped up to clap Ladden on the back.

"Ernie—" Ladden began.

"Be careful, though." Ernie held up a beefy finger. "Ladden here breaks hearts as often as I break wind."

"Ernie!" Ladden said sternly. *"Do* you mind?" Glaring at his uncle, he jerked his head in a motion that said, "Scram," but the man was unfazed.

"Actually, Mr. Sanderson," Jasmine said, holding back a smile, "I'm looking for a pay phone to locate my impounded car."

"Give me your tag number and I'll make the call from the bar phone," Ladden offered.

Jasmine smiled her thanks and rummaged in her purse for something to write on.

"Here," Ladden said, extending the scrap of paper in his hand. "You can write on the back."

"Another love note from one of the waitresses?" Ernie asked, peering over his shoulder.

Ladden frowned. "Ernie, why don't you—"

"Take Jasmine with me to watch Maddie open her presents?" Ernie cut in smoothly, then gently clasped her elbow and flashed a glowing smile. "I'd love to. How about it, little lady?"

Jasmine shrugged awkwardly. "Well—"

"Silvie makes the best punch you ever tasted," Ernie cajoled. "Her secret ingredient is cranberry ginger ale."

Ladden exhaled noisily. His face grew redder by the second. She wanted to rescue him.

"Ernie, I don't think Jasmine—"

"It sounds fun," she said quickly. "I haven't had good punch in a long time."

Ernie smiled smugly at his nephew. "We'll be in the back when you're finished."

Jasmine allowed herself to be led away with a

backward glance at a bewildered looking Ladden. They threaded their way toward the far corner of the dining room where about twenty people were gathered around a beaming young girl with long, honey-colored hair. Ernie waved his hands and the group quieted, studying her with curious eyes.

"Everyone," he said proudly, "this is Jasmine, *Ladden*'s friend."

The inflection in his voice, coupled with his wagging eyebrows garnered a collective, singsongy "Ah" from the group that brought warmth to her cheeks. An attractive, plump, middle-aged woman stepped forward and kissed Jasmine on both cheeks. "Welcome, my dear. I'm Silvie, Ladden's aunt. My daughter Maddie was just getting ready to open her birthday gifts."

"I don't want to intrude," Jasmine said uncomfortably. They obviously thought she was Ladden's girlfriend.

"Nonsense," Silvie said, leading her to a chair. "You look familiar to me—are you a model or something?"

Jasmine laughed. "No, I'm an interior designer. I've been shopping at Ladden's Castle for years."

Silvie squinted. "Maybe I've seen your picture somewhere."

Her picture had appeared regularly in the lifestyle section of the newspaper since she had begun dating the governor, but she didn't want to bring it up. "I suppose I just have one of those faces."

The woman dismissed the subject with a wave. "Let me get you a nice cup of punch."

Jasmine settled between Ruby, Silvie's niece, and Joey, Ladden's cousin who, she discovered in a few minutes, owned a third of the tavern. Joey, a short, dark-haired fellow who looked to be a few years older than Ladden, seemed to be keenly interested in her legs. Ladden wasn't in her direct line of vision, and she resisted the urge to crane her neck lest she incite the group. She sipped her punch and watched in silence as Maddie opened a stack of presents, exclaiming with glee over in-line skates from her parents, a jewelry box from an aunt, and a charm bracelet from her Uncle Ladden.

"Oh, it's beautiful," the little girl gasped, holding out the bracelet for everyone to see. She looked around the tavern. "Where is Uncle Ladden?"

"He's making some phone calls for me," Jasmine said, touched that he'd bought such a lovely gift for his niece and feeling worse and worse for making him miss the festivities. She slipped an embellished pewter comb from her braided hair. "I didn't know to bring a gift, Maddie, but I'd like you to have this."

"Wow," Maddie breathed, stroking the comb. "Will you show me how to fix my hair like yours sometime?"

After a slight hesitation, she responded, "Of

c-course—the next time I see you." She felt more
and more out of place.

"Are you going to marry Uncle Ladden?" the
girl asked, eliciting laughter from the adults.

Ladden approached the table, and from the
look on his face Jasmine was sure he had heard his
niece's question. "Jasmine and I are just friends,
Maddie." He threw the adults a warning look.

"Thanks for the bracelet, Uncle Ladden."

"You're welcome." He walked around behind
Maddie and dropped a kiss on the top of her head.

"Look what Jasmine gave me," she said, lifting
the comb for his inspection.

"Very nice." He nodded appreciatively, swinging his gaze in her direction. Jasmine squirmed,
torn by the urge to flee the intimacy of the atmosphere and the desire to observe a normal, all-
American family—a phenomenon she had never
experienced.

As Maddie opened the last of her gifts, Ladden
moved behind Jasmine's chair and whispered, "I
found your car. It's in city lot D, but you can't
claim it until morning."

She frowned, but she had feared as much.
Pushing back her chair, she said, "Well, I guess I'd
better be getting home." She answered the chorus
of good-byes as she left the table, all too aware that
Ladden was only a step behind her.

"Er, Jasmine, I'm sorry you got dragged into
all that." He gestured vaguely toward the party.
"My family can be a little exuberant."

"It's okay," she said, moving as quickly as possible toward the bar.

"I'll take you home."

She stopped and slowly turned back to see him rubbing his hands together in a nervous gesture. Her heart jumped erratically. "I don't think—"

"I'll go back to the shop and get the truck—"

"No!" Her tone was more sharp than she'd intended, triggered by alarm she felt at the attraction that had sprung up between them.

Ladden wet his lips, then nodded and took a step back. His smile was apologetic. "That's okay—I didn't expect you to want to go rattling around in my big truck."

Jasmine winced inwardly when she realized she'd hurt his feelings. The world could use more people like Ladden—he was a true gentleman. "I mean, no, don't do that because . . . because it's a nice night." She conjured up a smile and waved toward the door. "I'll walk with you."

"Yeah?" he said, the right side of his mouth climbing.

"Yeah."

"W-Would you like to get a drink first?"

She shook her head. "I'm already running late."

"Okay, sure." He swept his arm toward the door.

She stepped ahead, inhaling sharply when his hand brushed her waist. He waved good-bye to his uncle, then held open the door for her. Jasmine gripped the lamp tightly to calm her pounding heart as she stepped down onto the sidewalk.

The night *was* lovely, she acknowledged as he fell into step beside her. The late October air was bracingly cool but fresh and head-clearing. Goose bumps skittered across her arms and shoulders beneath the thin silk of her tunic. The streetlights flickered on, activated by the falling dusk, and a few pedestrians dotted the sidewalks in small knots, on their way to the movies or to dinner. Traffic had slowed, almost as if it were lulled by the haunting sounds of a saxophonist on the corner. They stopped to listen for a few seconds, and Ladden tossed a bill into his upturned hat.

"You have a nice family," Jasmine ventured into the silence between them.

He chuckled, shaking his head. "Thanks—they can be a bit overwhelming, but they're great. Silvie and Ernie practically raised me—Maddie is more like my little sister than my niece." His voice held true warmth, and she felt a stab of envy. "It was nice of you to give her the comb."

"She seems like a sweet kid."

"The best. And she really liked you—they all did."

She smiled. "That's because they thought I was your girlfriend."

His laughter was short and rueful. "Sorry about that. My aunt and uncle are anxious for me to settle down."

Jasmine grinned. "Well, according to your uncle, you have your pick of women."

"My uncle is delusional."

They walked a little farther before she asked, "So why haven't you married, Ladden?"

He pursed his lips. "I guess you could say I'm married to my job. I work long hours, and I spend most of my time away from the business scavenging for more antiques."

"But I'd think having . . . someone . . . around to help you would make things easier."

His smile was easy, displaying white, even teeth. "If by *someone* you mean a wife, well, I simply haven't met a woman who shares my love for old things."

She scoffed. "But what about the shop? Everyone who comes in loves old things."

Ladden shook his head. "Most of my clients are gay men"—he sighed dramatically and pinned her down with his gaze—"or unavailable women."

Her stomach seemed to be doing funny things. "Th-there are lots of single women in Sacramento," she stammered as he led her down the dimly lit alley beside his store. Their footsteps echoed off the brick pavement, and she heard scurrying noises near the Dumpster, driving her closer to his side.

"Except I'm not interested in lots of single women," he said, putting his hand on her waist. He swung open the door of his big delivery truck. "I'm interested in a *particular* single woman."

Jasmine's breath left her as she read the seriousness in Ladden's gaze. He towered over her by a good ten inches, and she had never considered herself a small woman. She dropped her gaze to his chest, which turned out to be a mistake, because the sight of his red shirt expanding with each breath sent her imagination running wild.

Her mind constructed words to explain that what he implied was impossible, to let him down gently—but the phrases were scrambled somewhere between her brain cells and her tongue. Instead, she allowed him to curl his hands around her waist and lift her—as easily as if she were one of those strange butterflies—into the seat of the roomy cab.

After he closed the door, Jasmine bit her tongue and counted to ten in the darkness. She'd call Trey the minute she arrived home and see if they could meet for dinner tomorrow, or maybe lunch—or even a snack. The driver-side door squeaked open, triggering the overhead light, and Ladden swung up into the seat. He banged the door shut three times before it stuck, then said, "I might ask you the same question." He pumped the gas pedal, then turned over the engine.

Intent on the calming effect of her counting, Jasmine asked, "What question?"

"Why haven't you married?"

She waited until he'd put the truck into gear and they'd lurched forward before she answered. "I've been waiting for the right man, I guess."

Ladden reached forward to turn on the radio. "And have you found the right man in Governor McDonald?"

Jasmine listened to the strains of a jazz guitar for several seconds, then said, "He's the most eligible bachelor in the state."

"So they say," he agreed. "Better buckle up."

"Are you a bad driver?" she teased, glad to change the topic.

"The shocks on this old truck have just about had it," he said with a grimace. "The seat belt will keep you from bouncing against the ceiling if we hit a pothole."

She laughed, relaxing into the soft, upholstered bench seat. The cavernous cab smelled like the lemon air freshener that dangled from one of the knobs on the imposing dashboard. Despite the seemingly endless space between her and Ladden, however, Jasmine felt the intimacy in sharing a confined space with a man who had so recently made her aware of his interest.

"I listened to the news for a report about the earthquake today," she said, trying to find safe conversational ground, "but I didn't hear a thing."

Even in the semidarkness, she sensed his unease. "I, uh, I guess the damage was confined to a small area."

"Were your losses substantial?"

"Quite a bit of glassware and a few clocks, but I'll survive."

"Good." She chanced a glance at his dark profile. "I'd hate to lose one of my most reliable resources."

He swung his gaze toward her. "If 'reliable' is all I can get, I guess I'll take it."

She laughed lightly, then realized they had come to a complete stop at an intersection and the light glowed green.

"Where do you live?" he asked, his tone sheepish.

Jasmine laughed harder. "Near the expressway, on Candlelight Court."

He whistled. "Nice area."

"I like it," she said, making a split-second comparison between her upscale condo and the hovel she'd lived in as a child.

"Do you have nice neighbors?"

Jasmine frowned into the darkness. Actually, she had no idea. "It's not a very social community—everyone's so busy, I suppose."

"I've been tempted to move a few times," Ladden said, "but every time I think of the possibility of getting stuck with bad neighbors, I stay put and count my blessings." He smiled at her across the seat. "Mr. and Mrs. Matthews keep their yard looking nice, and the Hanovers are always inviting me over to cook out with them."

"Sounds homey," she agreed, thinking a murder could be committed in the unit next to hers and she'd never know it. "So, have you decided on a price for the rug?"

He probed his cheek with his tongue. "I still haven't decided whether to sell it."

"Just promise me I'll get first crack at it," she cajoled.

"*If* I decide to sell the rug, you'll get first crack at it."

"I'm making headway," she said triumphantly.

Inclining his head toward the bag she clung to, he said, "By the way, the check you gave me for that copper lamp was way too much. I can't accept it."

"Just put it on my account," she said quickly, thinking that, after the quake, he could probably use a little cash flow. "Will you be open for business tomorrow?"

"Only for you." He smiled, sending little tremors to her midsection. "Otherwise, I'll be closed to finish the cleanup and complete my inventory."

She suddenly wished she hadn't accepted his generosity. What would Trey say if he knew she accepted a ride home from another man? Her heart tripped double time, and she glanced into the side mirror. What if a photographer were following them at this very minute? She could just imagine the scandal in the papers.

"I'll be needing that table in a few days," she said in a shaky voice. "Pencil in the delivery to the governor's mansion whenever it's convenient."

"You've been working on the governor's place for a long time—what, eight months now?"

"Seven," she corrected. "I hadn't planned on

being asked to overhaul the private quarters once I finished the public touring areas."

"What a lucky break," he said lightly.

She glanced at him sideways. "Yes."

"I saw you on the news the other night at a fund-raiser. You looked nice."

Jasmine shifted restlessly, wondering why she felt compelled to defend herself. "I do what I can to help Trey's reelection campaign."

"Do you think he'll win?"

"I certainly hope so," she said, then added, "and not just for his sake. I truly believe he's the best man for the job."

"He made a lot of enemies when he went head-to-head with the logging industry."

"That took a lot of guts."

Ladden made a clicking sound with his cheek. "And his campaign is taking a lot of money—close to three million I heard?"

"Trey thinks it's worth it," she murmured. She herself found it difficult to imagine the dollars people at Trey's level bandied about as if it were milk money.

They hit a pothole, bounced up, and landed with enough force to jar her teeth. She laughed and he apologized.

"You might want to mention that little bump in the road the next time you see the governor," he teased. "I've called my councilman twice and got nowhere."

"Take a right at the next light," she said. "Then turn into the gate."

He slowed the truck at the gated entrance and rolled down the window. Jasmine leaned forward and waved to the guard. The man glanced at the truck with a puzzled look but waved them on through.

"Seems like a safe place," Ladden remarked.

"Mine is the third unit on the left," she said, then unbuckled her belt, poised to make her getaway as soon as possible. He pointed to her condo for clarification, and she nodded. "Thanks for the ride," she said cheerfully. She lifted the door handle, but it refused to budge.

"The handle sticks," Ladden said with a little smile. "I'll have to get it from the outside."

He opened the door and jumped down. Jasmine sat in the dark and tried to get a handle on the absurd feelings echoing in her chest. She had to distance herself from this man who, by some collision of hormones and timing, had caught her completely off guard.

He opened the complaining passenger door and raised his arms to help her down. Jasmine opened her mouth to decline, but with one look at his sincere, gentle smile, her will dissolved. She settled one hand on his shoulder. His big hands practically spanned her waist, his thumbs pressing on either side of her navel as he swung her to the ground.

For a few seconds, her hand seemed glued to

his shoulder, his hands bound to her waist. Thankfully, he moved first, clearing his throat. "I'll walk you to your door."

"There's no need," she said quickly.

His mouth curved into an innocent smile. "My aunt would never forgive me if I displayed such a lapse in manners."

She relented and walked toward the well-lit entrance of her townhouse. As she dug for her keys, Jasmine decided she couldn't blame her knocking knees on Ladden—she was more afraid of herself. What if he tried to kiss her good night? Would she let him? Would she like it?

He walked a half-step behind her, his boots scraping against the sidewalk. At her door she turned around and offered him a broad smile. "Thanks for seeing me home," she said, a bit too loudly.

"No problem," he said, then leaned forward and, before she had time to react, grazed his warm cheek against hers—just his cheek. "Good night," he murmured.

Jasmine had the feeling that if he'd been wearing a hat, he would have doffed it to her, but instead he simply nodded, turned on his heel, and strode back to his big, ugly truck, whistling.

After fumbling with her keys, she finally unlocked the door and disabled the security alarm. But she couldn't do anything to silence the warning alarms going off in her head. She leaned against the door, willing herself not to watch him pull away from the curb, but she couldn't resist. Jasmine tiptoed into the dark living room and fingered aside the curtain, smiling as he backed up the truck, its bulky shape nearly outlined with tiny safety lights. After some tight maneuvering, he managed to turn the truck around on the narrow street and pull away, the aged vehicle coughing and sputtering.

She bit her lower lip and told herself the events of the last few hours meant nothing. When she realized she was holding the lamp with a white-knuckled grip, she scoffed at herself and unwrapped her new treasure. After setting the lamp beneath the spotlight on the mantel, she stepped back to admire the little pot, then adjusted it to the right. On impulse, she lifted the tiny lid, then stepped back in amazement as butterflies burst through the opening and fluttered toward the ceiling. Somehow, the insects from Ladden's store must have been trapped inside.

Incredulous, Jasmine gaped as they spread throughout her living room, then she laughed through her fingers. When Ladden's easy smile appeared in her mind, confusion, excitement, and wonder crowded her chest. She sat down hard on her leather couch in the dark and hugged a cushion under her chin as she watched the butterflies gravitate to the spotlight over the mantel.

Ladden waited until he guided his big, rickety truck through the gates of the posh community before he allowed himself an ear-to-ear grin. He pounded the steering wheel and whooped as he pulled onto the expressway. But after a few minutes of driving, he pictured the groomed landscaping in front of Jasmine's expensive townhouse, looked around the smelly cab of his old truck, and plummeted back to earth.

Jasmine dated the governor, and even if McDonald didn't win reelection, he would still be a powerful man. And she was a successful woman in her own right, with a thriving business and a nice home in the most plush area of town. She'd have no use for a man whose social circle rarely extended past family and neighbors. In a word, she was . . . untouchable—to him, at least.

A radio ad to vote for Trey McDonald sounded over the aged dashboard speakers. Ladden switched the station and sighed. "I wish Jasmine could *see* how crazy I am about her," he muttered. "Before it's too late."

FIVE

Despite the mixed feelings raging through his head and heart the night before, Ladden woke with a smile on his face. A full-body stretch still left room to spare in his knotty pine sleigh bed. He grabbed a pillow and rolled to his side, imagining Jasmine lying next to him, her hair splayed over the white pillowcase. Then he forced himself to forget his musings. A casual ride home did not a relationship make.

He swung his feet to the pale wood floor and scrubbed his hands over his face. Wriggling his toes against the smooth, cool planks, he pondered the addition of the antique rug to his bedroom. He glanced around the comfortably cluttered room, thinking the carpet might actually lend some sense of order to his eclectic collection of furnishings. And it might give him some incentive to put up a curtain or two, he thought, frowning at the bare windows. On an inspired Sunday afternoon several months ago, he had hung the old metal rods he'd bought because he liked the primitive fish finials, but he'd never gotten around to hanging curtains. The view into his backyard was too nice to cover up, anyway, he thought as he pulled himself to his feet and walked over to the window in his boxers.

Okay, so maybe the daffodils needed to be thinned—they were looking a bit wild—and maybe the roses could use a trim—they were buckling the wall trellises—but it made for a private little paradise he'd enjoyed creating over the past seven years he'd lived in the Glenhayden house. He saluted his lonely looking hammock and made a silent promise to relax this weekend, once the store was back in order.

The thought of the mysterious earthquake and the damage it had wrought dampened his spirits somewhat. If he hadn't experienced other tremors growing up in Sacramento, he might give credence to other explanations . . . but he knew an earthquake when he felt one, and he was going to stick by his story, no matter how unbelievable it seemed.

He showered and shaved with less speed than usual, picturing Jasmine's golden skin and black braid vividly enough to cause his body to harden. After some teeth-grinding and cold water, he left the bathroom, pulled on a pair of worn jeans and a T-shirt, then padded into the kitchen to turn on the coffeemaker. While the dark liquid brewed, he fixed a couple of slices of raisin toast and straightened his small kitchen. Betsy would be over during the day to clean for the week, but he hated to leave *too* much of a mess.

Betsy, his curvy, red-haired housecleaner, had made it clear she wouldn't mind going to dinner with him sometime, but he needed a reliable housecleaner more than he needed a date. He frowned as he carried a small breakfast tray outside to his customary spot on the front porch. Maybe he should give up this ridiculous fantasy about Jasmine Crowne and get serious about finding a woman who wanted to share his life.

He set the tray on a glass-topped, wrought-iron table, then wiped the dew from one of the matching chairs. Barefoot, he loped off the porch and down the short flight of stone steps to the end of the cobblestone sidewalk where the practiced paperboy typically left the *Daily News.*

"Hello, Ladden," Mrs. Matthews called from next door.

He lifted his hand in a friendly wave, smiling at her brightly colored robe. She scooped up her paper and disappeared inside the house where she and her husband had lived for more than twenty years. Ladden turned and scrutinized the front of his home, critically comparing the worn red brick, jutting dormers, and wide, inviting porch to the sleek lines of Jasmine's pale-colored townhouse. Her tiny yard was professionally landscaped. And although his sprawling lawn was neatly clipped, his homey vegetation was out of control. English ivy practically obscured the white block foundation under the porch and boldly encroached on the wood railing.

A house, he'd always thought, told a lot about the person who lived there. Which only reinforced his observation that he and Jasmine were polar opposites. He was a shabby brick home, full of thoughts as old-fashioned as his furniture, and she was an upscale condominium, safely gated against the likes of him.

He slowly unfolded the newspaper to scan the headlines, then stumbled and stubbed his toe on an uneven stone in the sidewalk. Cursing and hopping, he stared at the bold headline that covered the entire first page: "A Wise Second Wish, Master."

The note the bartender handed him last night at Tabby's flashed before his eyes. "*Some guy with a turban,*" Malone had said.

With shaking hands, Ladden climbed the steps and fell into his chair, unable to look at the paper. He downed the cup of coffee before he took a deep breath and smoothed open the front page. To his dismay, the headline had not changed. His fingers tingled and he felt light-headed. The rest of the paper looked normal—weather, movie reviews, obituaries, but the front page . . .

"What the heck is going on?" he mumbled. Ladden lunged off the porch and marched through the grass to the Matthewses' front door.

Mrs. Matthews answered his slightly frantic knock. "Ladden, how good to see you. Won't you come in and join me for oatmeal?"

"Thanks, Mrs. Matthews," he said, feeling foolish. "But I was wondering if I could see your paper." He shrugged. "M-mine was missing the front page."

She disappeared, then came back and extended the paper with a smile. "Harmon isn't up yet, so just drop it off before you leave for work."

With his heart thudding, he opened the paper and glanced over the headline that announced Governor McDonald trailed his opponent in the polls by a growing margin. Ladden inhaled and exhaled slowly, then folded the paper and handed it back to his neighbor. "Th-thanks anyway, Mrs. Matthews. It looks like more of the same old stuff."

"You're right." She sighed and wagged her graying head. "It appears the governor is going to lose the race for sure. Too bad, I think he's a nice young man, don't you?"

Ladden swallowed hard and nodded, offering what he hoped was a convincing smile. "Y-yeah." He backed away slowly, barely restraining the urge to bolt. "Tell Harmon hello for me, Mrs. Matthews."

He waded through the damp grass, ignoring the wetness oozing between his toes and climbing the legs of his jeans. "There's something weird going on here," he mumbled, squashing the panic that ballooned in his chest. His newspaper lay scattered on his porch, strewn by the wind. He gathered up the flimsy, damp sheets, but now the front page really was missing. Ladden scoured the yard, searched the neighbors' bushes, and looked up into trees, to no avail.

Running inside, Ladden raced to his bedroom, yanked the shirt he'd worn last night off the floor and rifled his pockets until he found the note the bartender had given him. He exhaled in relief when he recognized Jasmine's handwriting where she'd written her car tag number. But when he turned over the crumpled note, the other side was blank . . . completely, absolutely, irrefutably blank.

By the time he locked up the house and climbed into his delivery truck, Ladden had convinced himself he'd close the store for a few days once he filed the insurance claim and drive down the coast for a short vacation. He'd been working too hard, and he was becoming consumed by a woman he couldn't have. Hell, he might even see if Betsy wanted to tag along—she was a good looking girl with a sweet disposition. And she came from a nice family on the outskirts of Glenhayden—hardworking people who wouldn't mind that he wasn't rich or influential.

In the daylight, his truck looked even worse than he remembered, and he tingled with embar-

Stephanie Bancroft
66

rassment when he realized that Jasmine was probably laughing at his clumsy efforts to be near her. By the time he pulled into the alley behind the store, he was determined to get out of Sacramento as soon as possible.

He opened the rear door to his storeroom and switched on the light, his gaze immediately drawn to the antique rug. Except it wasn't lying on the table where it had been last night when he'd locked up—he was standing on it.

The tiny hairs on the back of his neck stood on end. He inhaled sharply when a handful of remaining butterflies, disturbed by his entry, took wing and fluttered around his head.

Pressing his lips together, Ladden took several calming breaths. There had to be a reasonable explanation. Perhaps another tremor had occurred during the night, flinging the rug across the room?

"Yeah," he muttered, nodding. "That's probably what happened." He took a step to the side on shaky knees, then bent and rolled up the carpet, his fingers stinging from the static electricity crackling across the wool surface. Lifting the tall bundle carefully, he carried it to a corner and stood it next to an armoire.

He backed away, eyeing the carpet warily. Then he opened the door to his showroom and flooded the area with light, expecting to see evidence of another tremor to support his theory. But things were exactly as he'd left them—not tidy— but unchanged.

His mind racing, Ladden walked through the shop slowly, stopping to lean on both hands against the long mahogany counter. He was imagining things: the note, the newspaper, the moving rug. Maybe the tremor *had* been an explosion of some kind, an explosion that had released fumes and claimed a few brain cells.

A knock on his door brought his head up. Mrs. Pickney stood on the other side of the glass door. He smiled in relief—he needed to have a sane conversation with a sane person. Ladden unlocked the door. "You're here early," he said.

"I wanted to talk to you before I opened, dear," Mrs. Pickney said, squeezing his hand.

"Is something wrong?"

She laughed. "Not at all. This won't take long—I'm retiring."

He blinked. "Retiring?"

"Yes. It occurred to me yesterday that you need the space, and I need to move on."

The business possibilities occurred to him instantly, but he spread his hands and slowly shook his head. "Mrs. Pickney, as much as I'd like to have your frontage, I'm afraid I'm not in a financial position to—"

"Ladden," she cut in, patting his hand. "I'm giving it to you."

He reached backward to steady himself on the counter. "You're what?"

"I'm giving it to you. I have no heirs. My sister and I have all the investments we'll ever need. Besides, you've kept up all the repairs for the last fifteen years—you've earned it."

He wondered briefly if she had lost her mind. Then he almost laughed aloud—if that wasn't the pot calling the kettle black. "Mrs. Pickney, I can't accept—"

"Ladden, this is my gift to you, my way of saying thanks for the friendship and support over the years." Her eyes shone. "You're like the son I never had. Nothing would make me happier than knowing I had helped you build your business."

Flabbergasted, he lifted his arms in the air. "I don't know what to say."

Her face creased in a wide smile. "Say you'll make Ladden's Castle a huge success."

He whooped and enfolded her in a bear hug, lifting her off the ground. "I will—I'll make it a huge success. Thank you!"

She laughed and kissed him on both cheeks. "I'll have my lawyer call you this afternoon to set up a time when we can transfer the deed." She waved as she headed for the door. "I need to call for a going-out-of-business permit."

Ladden watched her leave, then sheer joy moved him to jump straight up in the air. As he landed, his words from the previous day floated back to him. *"I wish Mrs. Pickney would simply retire and give me her space."*

He dropped heavily into the leather chair behind his counter, laid his head back, and reflected on the strange events of the last twenty-four hours. The craziness had all started when he'd carried in that mysterious rug.

Ladden squinted. What was it the guy had said to him? *"The spell has been broken . . . You have given me my life . . . Anything you want, simply wish for it, and I shall grant you three of your heart's desires . . ."*

He stared at the ceiling and shook his head. "That's too bizarre to even consider," he said. Yet he *had* wished for the fantastic, incredible thing that had just occurred.

"Coincidence," he murmured. Mrs. Pickney was giving him her building because she had no family and because he had helped her over the years. Not because he had wished for it.

The note from the bar! *"A wise first wish, Master."* And his paper's strange headline: *"Wise second Wish, Master."* But even if he were to give an ounce of credence to the wild ravings of a homeless man, he couldn't for the life of him recall wishing for anything besides Mrs. Pickney's store space.

The peal of the telephone broke his train of thought. Grateful for the diversion, Ladden jammed his fingers through his hair, then picked up the handset.

"Ladden's Castle," he said politely.

"Is this Ladden Sanderson?" a man asked.

"Yes, may I help you?"

"Is this the same Ladden Sanderson who rented all the billboards on the bypass?"

Ladden frowned. "Billboards?"

"Yeah—the ones that say, 'Ladden Sanderson is crazy about Jasmine Crowne.'"

SIX

Jasmine angled her head at the TV, watching one of Trey's political commercials. Tall, slim, and handsome, he was a commanding yet comforting figure, with serious eyes and a strong chin. During the time they'd spent together, she had been pleasantly surprised by Trey McDonald's sincere regard for his duty as an elected figure.

"How lucky I am," she murmured, plaiting her hair into a long, loose braid. The frustration she had harbored last night when he hadn't returned her page dissolved as the camera zeroed in for a close-up.

"Vote for me," he said with a nod and a smile, "and I'll make sure your voice is louder than the lobbyists who are trying to take over state government."

She sighed. Trey was a very busy man, with an agenda far more important than keeping his girlfriend entertained. He was trying to change the world, and she was pouting because he didn't have time to take her to the movies. *Shame on me.*

The cordless phone gurgled. Jasmine lifted the handset to her ear.

"Hello?"

"Good morning, beautiful."

She clutched the phone tighter and smiled. "Trey."

"Sorry I didn't get back to you last night. I simply couldn't get away from Senator Dodd until after midnight, and I didn't want to disturb your sleep."

"Are you insinuating that I need my beauty sleep?" she teased.

"Never," he said. "Could I persuade you to attend a dinner and rally with me this evening?"

"Possibly," she said, her voice light.

His chuckle rumbled over the line. "I'd consider it a huge favor. It's a big media event, and maybe the press will be more kind if I have you by my side—you're so good at working those vultures. And you're so damned photogenic."

"Hmmm," she murmured. "Sounds like you need a prop."

"I miss you," he said, his voice deepening. "Once this campaign is over, I promise I'll make it up to you. We'll go away for the weekend."

She immediately felt contrite. "Trey, you don't have to make it up to me. I know the election means everything to you." She smiled into the receiver. "And it means everything to me, too."

"You're a gem. Then I'll see you tonight?"

"Absolutely. Where?"

"The Shoalt Hotel, seven-thirty. I won't be able to pick you up, but I'll send over a car."

Remembering her transportation predicament, she cleared her throat. "That's not necessary, but speaking of cars, I have a confession to make. Mine was towed last night."

He laughed. "You're kidding."

"I could have sworn the parking meter still had time left on it—"

"Don't worry about it. Do you know where it is?"

"City lot D," she said morosely.

"No problem—I'll make a few phone calls—"

"Trey," she cut in, "I just want you to be aware of the situation." She laughed softly. "If you took care of this, and someone found out, the media would blow it way out of proportion."

He sighed. "As petty as it sounds, you're probably right."

"I already called a taxi, so I'll pick up my car in an hour or so. I hope this doesn't embarrass you."

"I'm sure the incident will go unnoticed, but thanks for being so concerned about how it might look. These days, it only takes a whiff of gossip to get a scandal started." He laughed dryly. "And right now I can't afford to lose a single vote."

"Things will turn around," she offered, a finger of guilt nudging her.

"I hope you're right. Will you still go out with me if I'm only an ex-governor?"

Jasmine laughed. "You don't sound very optimistic this morning."

"Have you seen this morning's headline? The numbers are pretty grim—oh, there's my other line. Are you sure I can't send over a car this evening?"

"No, I'll drive," she assured him. "See you tonight."

With shaking hands, she set down the phone. Trey's words about scandal echoed in her head. How foolish she had been last night. Even though nothing had happened, if a photographer had been inclined to mischief, a photo of Ladden Sanderson dropping her off at her apartment would be easy to exaggerate. She glanced over at the unfolded paper and swallowed hard. Such a photo would have sold more papers than the news that the incumbent governor was falling behind in the polls.

Jasmine quickly fastened the end of her braid with a silver clasp, then stepped into pumps and walked to the tiny kitchen. Of the sparse contents of her refrigerator, orange juice looked like the safest choice. Her stomach still churned over her physical and emotional brush with Ladden, and she decided the best course of action would be to avoid contact with him until she got her head back on straight. An evening with Trey would do wonders. But when she wandered back into the living room, the copper lamp drew her to the mantel, and she felt an uncomfortable twinge of longing for Ladden's easy smile. A single black-and-orange butterfly sat perched on the blade of the silent ceiling fan.

"I'm bringing a net home with me," she said, shaking a warning finger at the insect.

Unable to resist, she lifted the lamp and ran her hands over the smooth, shiny copper. When she felt raised etchings, she moved to the window and squinted at the scratchings near the bottom. "Arabic," she murmured, amazed that she could even recognize a letter or two because she hadn't studied the alphabet of her mother's lineage since she was very young. The full words escaped her, however, and she resolved to unearth the old textbooks buried somewhere in her attic.

Frowning, she fought the sadness that filled her chest when she thought about her childhood. Her mother, gone now for over twenty years, would be happy to know she was thinking about the old language, no matter how flimsy the excuse. Running her fingers over the cool metal surface, she smiled at the source of the unlikely link to her heritage.

A car horn interrupted her reverie. Jasmine ran out the front door and hopped into the backseat of the cab. She leaned forward to give the driver directions, then stopped at the sight of his black turban. He looked strangely familiar. "Do I know you from somewhere?" she asked.

The skinny man shook his head. "No. Just arrived in city."

She nodded, wondering how on earth the man could drive with all that fabric draped around his body. But he seemed to understand where she told him to go, so she sat back and flipped through her calendar, planning her day. She had written herself a note to schedule delivery of the table Ladden had refinished for her. Always conscientious, Ladden would remember.

Jasmine still wished she could talk him into selling her that carpet—it would be the perfect congratulatory gift for Trey. With a sigh, she decided that despite the little awkwardness that had sprung up between her and Ladden, she needed to stay in touch if she was going to get her hands on that rug. When guilt pricked her conscience, she squashed it. After all, she was willing to pay him a goodly sum.

She planned to spend most of the day at the office building of a telecommunications company she had acquired as a customer only last week. The company president, a young, aggressive woman, had challenged her to give the offices a cutting edge decor, an atmosphere to match their progressive philosophy. Jasmine's mouth twisted into a wry smile. Lots of metal and glass—at least she wouldn't need to shop at Ladden's Castle for this job.

"A wonderful day," the cabdriver said, glancing at her in the rearview mirror.

Jasmine nodded and looked out the window, realizing for the first time that it was the beginning of another gorgeous day in Sacramento. How she loved it here where winter was comically short and spring practically unending. And the city's landscape was evolving beautifully. The recent retail development on the bypass was being carefully tended with lots of green space retained, restrictions on high-rises, limited billboards—

She jerked forward and pressed her nose against the window, unable to believe her eyes. All moisture left her mouth, and her lips parted to drag in more oxygen. "Slow down!" she cried, holding a hand over her heart. This wasn't happening. She wasn't staring out the window at more than a dozen billboards fading over the horizon that proclaimed in yellow letters on a black background, "Ladden Sanderson is crazy about Jasmine Crowne."

The cabdriver leaned forward, grinning at the signs. "Is lucky woman, no?"

She sank back into the seat, her hand on her forehead. Colored lights flashed behind her eyelids. "No," she whispered. *What* was Ladden thinking? *What* was she going to tell Trey? She gulped for air as perspiration gathered around her hairline. Would this affect his campaign? Her stomach lurched sickeningly. Of course it would affect his campaign.

Clawing for her cellular phone, Jasmine stopped. Who would she call first? Ladden? Trey?

Her heart hammered against her breastbone, and she laid her head back. Maybe she should tell the driver to just keep going until they reached Ohio—somewhere she could disappear without a trace. Before she had time to decide, her phone rang. She stared at it, clutching the handset until three rings had expired. Then with a deep breath, she punched a button. "H-hello?"

"Ms. Crowne?"

At the sound of her assistant's voice, Jasmine's shoulders sagged in relief. "April."

"I hate to disturb you, Ms. Crowne, but the phones are going crazy—newspapers, TV reporters." She lowered her voice. "Even the governor's office. Something about billboards?"

Her mind spun. What could she say? "Oh, my God."

"And that nice Mr. Sanderson called, but he sounded frantic—he said he needed to speak to you *immediately.*"

"April," she said evenly, taking deep breaths. "Whatever you do, don't give this number to anyone."

"I won't."

"If anyone else calls, tell them the billboards are a simple misunderstanding and take down their name."

"Yes, ma'am, but what should I do about the crowd that's gathering outside?"

Jasmine closed her eyes. "C-crowd?"

"I locked the door, but they're banging on it

nonstop. You can probably hear it in the background."

"Oh, my God."

"You already said that, Ms. Crowne."

"April, I won't be coming in today," Jasmine managed to croak. "I'll call you later." Weakly, she punched a button to disconnect the call, then stabbed in the number to Ladden's Castle. But his recorder clicked on. "Ladden," she said, as lightly as she dared, "this is Jasmine. There seems to be some misunderstanding about our, uh, relationship, and I really need to talk to you. I'll call you later." A shiver tickled her spine when she thought about how much she had trusted him last night . . . and she felt absurdly saddened by the realization that Ladden Sanderson might be a little off his antique rocker. And she was just a tiny bit flattered that he would make his crush so public.

Before she had time to consider this revelation, her phone rang again.

"Hello?" she ventured.

"Hello again, my dear," Trey said smoothly. His voice sounded cheerful—a bit *too* cheerful. "I'm sitting in a traffic jam on the bypass. It seems everyone is stopping to gawk at some very interesting billboards. Maybe I'm mistaken, but I thought we had an understanding. Is there something you'd like to tell me?"

Her stomach quailed. "I . . . I . . ." She manufactured a laugh that came out sounding high-pitched and a little hysterical. "Oh, that Ladden. What a kidder he is."

"So this, this . . . *kidder*—he's an acquaintance of yours?"

"A business acquaintance," she supplied quickly. "He owns an antiques store on Pacific and often finds me special pieces." She laughed again, sounding slightly less squeaky. "He's holding a table now that I'd like to put in the small conference room in the Winchester wing." Jasmine knew she was rambling, but she couldn't stop. "In fact, he has a rug I think would look great in your b-bedroom."

"Oh, really?" he asked, his voice teasing. "Why do I get the feeling this Sanderson guy is trying to pull the rug out from under *me?*"

"We're strictly friends," she assured him, rolling her shoulders as her underarms grew moist. "I'm sure the billboards are some kind of joke."

"Well, he has a lousy sense of timing." Trey's voice grew softer. "Jasmine, are you sure there isn't something going on between the two of you? I can't deny that I'd be very hurt, but I'd rather know now than be embroiled in some kind of love triangle scandal."

The warm, fuzzy feeling Ladden had evoked in her last night barbed through her chest. "No, Trey," she asserted. "There is absolutely nothing going on between me and Ladden Sanderson."

"Good," he said, his good mood seemingly restored. "But the reporters will probably shadow us tonight. Do you think you can force yourself to occasionally throw adoring glances my way?"

She smiled into the phone. "I think I can manage that."

"Wear something red."

Jasmine said good-bye, then pushed a button with a shaky finger to disconnect the call. She longed for a few quiet hours to sort through the emotions ricocheting through her, but she realized nothing would be resolved until she spoke with Ladden.

"This is it, no?" the driver asked.

With a jolt, Jasmine looked up and saw they had indeed arrived at the city impound lot. She paid the little man, took a deep breath, and entered the government office. To her amazement, the clerk accepted her payment and released her car without comment or raised eyebrows. Feeling marginally better, she handed a copy of the release to the attendant, then walked stiffly to her car. But just as she inserted her key, a voice split the air.

"Ms. Crowne, over here!"

She jerked her head toward the sound, then froze when she saw a lone camera with a large lens pointed in her direction.

"Say cheese."

She could hear the whirring succession of photos being taken as the man twisted his shoulders for different angles. Her tongue would not move.

At last he paused. "Care to make a statement, Ms. Crowne?"

"About what?" she sputtered, putting on as brave a face as she could muster.

"About how the governor's neglect has driven you into the arms of a blue-collar lover?"

"That's ridiculous," she stammered.

The man smirked. "Not according to the guard at the complex where you live. You really should be more discreet, Ms. Crowne."

Ladden gripped the steering wheel of Mrs. Pickney's car and eased it onto the shoulder of the bypass.

"Holy Mary, Mother of God," he breathed. "I'm in the Twilight Zone." But the line of billboards that stretched before him were all too real. Yesterday most of them had encouraged citizens to vote for Governor Trey McDonald. Today they all announced that the governor's girlfriend was being pursued by an idiot.

He climbed out of the car on shaky legs, still unable to believe his eyes. How had this happened?

Ladden raked his hand through his hair. A shudder of fear traveled his spine as the words he'd muttered last night on the way home finally came back to him. "*I wish Jasmine could see how crazy I am about her.*"

He swallowed hard, shaking his head. No way.

There were no such things as magic lamps and mobile carpets and genies and wishes. Yet his paper's headline taunted him. *"Wise Second Wish, Master."* He leaned heavily against the car. He was absolutely, positively losing his mind.

"Greetings, Master."

Ladden jerked his head around, straightening when he saw the skinny homeless man from his store, swathed in yards of pale fabric and still sporting his black turban. The man looked completely at ease, as if he often passed time at the base of a billboard. Ladden's mouth twisted—the oddball probably did.

"You," he said, striding toward the man, "have some explaining to do."

The man grinned, revealing white, gapped teeth. "Your lady saw the signs this morning. She was quite surprised."

Ladden's stomach lurched. "No more surprised than I was." He tried to keep his voice calm. He was, after all, dealing with a maniac. "Or, I wager, her boyfriend," he added dryly. Then he frowned. "How do you know she saw them?"

Another grin. "I was with her, of course."

"Of course," Ladden said.

"My last master wasted his wishes foolishly," the man said with a sad face. Then he brightened. "But you . . . you are a good man with a big heart and—how you say—a big head?" He tapped his finger to his temple.

Ladden pursed his lips. "I hope you mean *smart.*"

"Ah, yes—smart," the man affirmed. "A wise master. Have you thought about your final wish?"

"Wait a minute." Ladden threw up his hands, shaking his head. "I am standing beside a busy highway talking to some kook with a turban who is trying to convince me he has the power to grant me anything I want."

The man frowned. "I cannot grant *any* wish. I am unable to take a life, to bring someone back to life, or to make someone fall in love." His face lit in another grin as he lifted a bony finger. "But I can help." He winked. "She is beautiful, your Jasmine. She reminds me of a princess I once knew."

"Okay, okay," Ladden said, clasping the man by his arm and steering him back to the car. "You're some rich lunatic who goes around eavesdropping on people and trying to make them happy. But I can assure you," he said sternly, waving back to the billboards, "this did not make *anyone* happy. Because of you, I am in deep hooey."

"Hooey?" the man asked.

"Horse shit," he clarified.

"Ah, camel dung," the man said, nodding.

Ladden sighed, guiding the man toward the passenger door. He waited for a break in the speeding traffic to climb in on the driver's side.

"Call whoever you have to call to get rid of those things," Ladden said as he turned over the ignition.

"They will be gone soon," the man promised.

"Good," he said as he pulled out on the highway. "Now I've got to come up with an explanation for Jasmine."

"Remember," the man said, when Ladden dropped him off in front of the homeless shelter a few minutes later. "A final wish—do not waste it."

Ladden smirked, then pulled away and drove as fast as he could to the rear entrance of his store. "Jasmine," he practiced, as he unlocked the back door, "you're not going to believe this, but—"

Ladden stopped, eyeing the carpet that once again lay draped over the table he was saving for Jasmine. He glanced at the corner where he had left it, rolled and standing on its end, then bit the inside of his cheek. He kept walking through the connecting door and into his showroom.

"But there's this madman with a turban who—"

He stopped again, glancing toward his front door where a crowd of people had gathered, including Uncle Ernie, Aunt Silvie, various other friends and relatives, and several photographers who were capturing the front of his store on film. His heart thudded in his chest as he unlocked the door to admit his uncle and aunt. Instead, a stocky, suited man pushed his way inside, then closed and locked the door behind him, shutting out Uncle Ernie and Aunt Silvie.

"Ladden Sanderson?" he barked.

Ladden frowned at the man and crossed his arms. "Yes."

The man flashed a badge, then shoved it back into his breast pocket. "Security, governor's office. Mr. Sanderson, if you so much as look at, talk to, or think about Jasmine Crowne again, you will be sorry. Is that understood?"

SEVEN

Ladden flicked his gaze over the stocky man standing before him. Inch for inch and pound for pound, they were a match. But with a badge and the weight of the governor's office behind him, the suited man had the upper hand, and by the smug look on his face, he knew it.

Ladden's mind raced as he considered the alternatives. He could deny he had anything to do with the billboards and risk looking like a fool, or he could lie and take responsibility for the ads and *prove* he was a fool.

Or he could try to turn the tables. And at this point, what did he have to lose? Certainly not his dignity. Assuming a wide-legged stance, he said, "I didn't catch your name, friend."

The man's expression remained stony. "Duncan, but I'm no friend."

Crossing his arms slowly, Ladden said, "Well,

Duncan, I didn't realize Governor McDonald was Ms. Crowne's personal keeper."

Duncan's left eyebrow rose a fraction. "Let's just say he's concerned about a very close acquaintance."

Ladden gave the man a tight smile. "Was this visit at the request of Ms. Crowne, or did the governor take it upon himself to come to her rescue?"

"I'm not at liberty to say."

Which meant Jasmine probably didn't know about it, he thought with a little zing of relief. "Funny, but I'm wondering what bothers the governor more—the fact that those billboards are directed toward a 'close acquaintance' of his, or the fact that the messages replaced his campaign ads."

Duncan narrowed his eyes and turned to leave. "Watch your step, Sanderson. Trey McDonald could buy and sell you a thousand times."

Despite the reality of the man's words, Ladden raised his voice after Duncan's retreating back. "That might be true, but I'll wager that Jasmine Crowne can't be bought."

With his hand on the doorknob, the bullish man turned and said, "Look, pal, I know she's a looker, but get real." He glanced around Ladden's messy showroom. "Do you honestly think the lady is going to dump the governor for this?"

Ladden frowned, stricken. The man was right, of course.

"Besides," Duncan said, his voice deceptively innocent. "I'd hate to see the fire marshal or the health inspector hanging around here all the time."

Anger sparked deep in his gut, but Ladden remained outwardly calm. "I run an honest business and I have nothing to hide," he told the man, spreading his hands wide.

"I was thinking more along the lines of your family's bar." Duncan's mouth twisted. "Cousins, I believe?"

"That sounds like extortion," he said between clenched teeth.

The man shrugged his thick shoulders. "Don't make it hard on yourself. If you ask me, the gov's doing you a favor—keeping you from humiliating yourself even more." Duncan jerked his head toward the crowd. "As for all those reporters out there, this billboard thing was a little joke that got out of hand, right?"

Ladden nodded slowly, biting the inside of his cheek.

"And you're a big supporter of the governor, right?"

Once again, Ladden nodded.

The man lowered his square chin. "And you'll stay away from Jasmine Crowne."

Ladden clenched his fists. "But she comes here all the time to buy furniture for her clients."

Duncan leaned toward him, shaking his head as if Ladden were dense. "This Crowne woman has her sights set on being the first lady of the state. You think she's going to risk that just to shop in some junk store?" The man snorted, then exited Ladden's Castle with a bang.

Ladden listened as the sound of the clanging bell faded, the noise obscured by the rising din of the crowd outside. His aunt pecked on the glass and waved. In a daze, he opened the door and held up his hands to stave off the swell of nearly two dozen bodies. Immediately, microphones were shoved in his face.

"Mr. Sanderson, are you having an affair with Governor McDonald's girlfriend?"

"Mr. Sanderson, how long have you been sleeping with Jasmine Crowne?"

"Mr. Sanderson, have you made a cuckold out of the most powerful man in the state?"

He winced, waving his aunt and uncle into the safety of the store. "This is a place of business, and I would appreciate it if you would all leave."

"Sir," a woman shouted, "will you comment on the billboards that link you romantically to Jasmine Crowne?"

He glanced at the cameras and saw Duncan standing in the back, apart from the crowd. Sweat popped out on his forehead. Although the odds of conjuring up any kind of smile under the circumstances seemed insurmountable, he forced the corners of his mouth upward and took a deep breath. "Ms. Crowne and I are . . . business associates. . . . I have acquired several pieces of antique furniture at her request for use in her clients' homes and businesses, including her recent job of refurbishing the governor's mansion." He swallowed hard before continuing. "The b-billboards are a practical joke between friends that got out of hand. I have the utmost respect for Governor Mc-Donald and I apologize if my, um, sense of humor has embarrassed either Ms. Crowne or the governor."

"Mr. Sanderson," the reporter persisted, "are you saying you're *not* interested in Jasmine Crowne?"

For one crazy instant, Ladden was tempted to say that yes, he was very much interested in Jasmine Crowne, that he loved her smile and her hair and the way her skin smelled, and that he'd be willing to challenge the power of the governor's office just to be near her . . . but he would be gambling with his cousins' business, painting himself as a nut, and Jasmine would never speak to him again—if indeed she would now, anyway. "I explained the nature of our relationship. I'm sorry if it isn't juicy enough for a scoop."

He ducked back into the store and locked the door, feeling nauseated. He desperately needed to get away from here. Although he rarely used the window blinds, he lowered the ones that worked, stirring up a good amount of dust and dimming the interior of the store.

"Beats all I ever did see," Ernie boomed, thumping Ladden on the back. A grin split his broad face as he informed Silvie, "He inherited my smarts, you know."

Ladden gasped for air while Silvie laughed. "Ernie drove me to work this morning and when he saw those signs, he nearly ran off the road." His aunt patted his arm. "It's very romantic, Ladden. I had no idea your Jasmine used to date the governor. No wonder she looked so familiar."

"Not used to," Ladden corrected, keeping his voice calm. "She still does."

Ernie whistled low. "Brass balls," he said with raw admiration. "You inherited those from me, too."

"My, it must have cost you a bundle," his aunt said, her voice singsongy.

"You can't imagine," Ladden muttered. His chances with Jasmine had gone from zero into the negative range.

"Business must be better than I thought," Ernie said. "Or are you counting on a big insurance settlement?"

He then realized in exasperation that he'd let the eccentric man who could verify his story about the earthquake slip through his fingers. "Trust me, Ernie, the billboards will be taken care of."

"What was Jasmine's reaction?" Silvie asked.

He ran his hand over his face. "I have no idea."

"You haven't talked to her?"

"Nope. Listen," he said, ushering them into the storeroom. "I know you two need to get to work. Maybe the rear entrance will be clear. And I'd appreciate it if you didn't talk to any reporters, okay?"

"All right," his aunt agreed hesitantly, clearly feeling left out. "Will you call me later and let me know what Jasmine—" She stopped, her brow furrowing. "What an unusual rug."

Ladden followed her finger and bit down hard on his tongue. The notorious rug lay draped over the collection of old trunks, a good ten feet from the table where he'd last seen it. "That, Aunt Silvie, is an understatement. I promise I'll call you later." He steered them out into the alley. A couple of spectators loitered even here, and a photographer stood, snapping his big truck from every angle. Shaking his head in frustration, Ladden slammed the door behind them, glared at the rug, then strode into the showroom to use the telephone. "Twenty-seven messages," he muttered.

Most of them were crank calls from relatives and friends, laughing uproariously over his stunt. He ground his teeth. Two radio stations requested live interviews, and someone from the headquarters of Trey McDonald's opponent seemed anxious to speak to him. But wedged between the nonsense was a call from the rug expert who said she would stop by the next day, and a brief message from Jasmine that sent his pulse climbing. He listened to her words six times, becoming more depressed with each replay. She sounded polite, yet mortified—and why wouldn't she be? His mind spun, wondering what on earth he was going to tell her.

Still holding the phone, Ladden sat down in a lumpy wing chair and stared into space. Never had

he felt quite so out of control. Between the mysterious earthquake, the generous gift from Mrs.
Pickney, the turbaned stranger, and all the hulla-
baloo surrounding Jasmine and the billboards, he
didn't have a clue what to do next.

A burgeoning headache he'd tried to ignore for
the last hour had finally battled its way to the surface, jackhammering his temples. If he were a serious drinking man, he'd be on his way to oblivion
right now. But he had the overwhelming fear that
if he turned his back on his predicament even for a
moment, something more bizarre might happen.

He sighed. Perhaps the sign company was the
best place to start. Maybe they would tell him who
had rented the billboards. Then at least he'd have a
name when he dropped by the shelter to see if the
man would sign an affidavit about the tremor. He
found the number in a tattered, stained phone
book, and a young man's voice came on the line
after the fourth ring.

"Capital Citywide Signs."

"This is Ladden Sanderson. I'm trying to—"

"Ah, Mr. Sanderson. Your money arrived this
morning."

"My money?"

"Yes, sir. Eighteen hundred dollars for eighteen billboards for one day." The man laughed.
"Kind of risky to send cash, don't you think? Do
you need a receipt?"

"N-no, thank you." Ladden chose his words

carefully. "How did you know the cash was from me?"

"The stationery envelope with your return address," the man said, his tone puzzled.

Ladden rummaged around on his desk and withdrew one of the off-white envelopes. He frowned. The old man must have lifted one before, during, or after the earthquake. One thing was sure, if the man had sent nearly two thousand dollars in cash through the mail, he had to be certifiably insane.

The young man broke into his reverie. "I spotted your messages on the way into the city this morning. Caused quite a traffic jam on the bypass. Caused quite an uproar around here, too. The boss is looking for the salesman who approved suspending the governor's ads for a day." The man made a clicking sound with his tongue. "Heads are going to roll over this one."

"You have my permission to return the governor's ads as soon as possible," Ladden assured him. "I think I've gotten more than enough exposure."

"Sure thing, Mr. Sanderson. We appreciate your business." The man chuckled. "And when you're ready to propose, we'll work with you."

Ladden frowned at the phone and hung up. It rang immediately, vibrating on his lap. He yanked up the handset, then wet his lips. "Hello?"

Jasmine's heart skipped a beat at the sound of his voice. She gripped the phone hard. He was just quiet, down-to-earth Ladden—the same man with whom she'd been doing business for years. What had changed? The fact that she had seen a more refined side to him? A glimpse of the gentleness beneath the coarse veneer?

"Hello?" he repeated, and she yanked her attention back to the phone call.

"Ladden, this is Jasmine."

"Oh . . . hello."

Silence stretched between them. She couldn't very well admit how flattered she felt that he would openly challenge someone as powerful as Trey McDonald for her affection. Although his methods were a bit old-fashioned—even prehistoric—she couldn't deny a zing of pleasure to think he'd gone to such extremes. Her brain formed words of protest, and she spoke at the same time he did.

"Ladden, about the billboards—"

"Jasmine, about the billboards—"

They both stopped, laughing. "Me first," she said. She inhaled deeply and ordered her pulse to slow. "I, um, always considered us friends, but if I've done anything to make you think that there's something between . . . I mean"—she exhaled—"I'm already involved with someone." Her skin tingled, and she was thankful he couldn't see her.

"Jasmine," his voice rumbled across the line, "most of the state knows who you're involved with." He sighed and she heard him fidgeting with the phone, as if he were walking . . . or pacing.

"I'm sorry about the billboards—a well-meaning acquaintance of mine thought it would be funny."

An odd sort of hurt found its way to her heart. "An acquaintance? You mean you didn't have anything to do with it?"

"Not really," he said with a small laugh. "And my friend seems to be a bit scarce right now, so I don't expect him to step forward and release us from this predicament." He sighed again. "I'm truly sorry, Jasmine. I hope his stunt didn't compromise your relationship with McDonald."

Flustered, Jasmine said quickly, "Don't worry about Trey. He trusts me. I told him our relationship was strictly business . . . th-that you have a rug I want for his private quarters."

"Which reminds me, my rug expert is dropping by tomorrow."

"Great," she said cheerfully, relieved that the conversation had turned in a more neutral direction. "Call me when you have a price."

"*If* I have a price," he corrected.

"If you have a price."

"I do need to deliver that table soon."

She pulled her lower lip into her mouth. "Um, I'm not sure if it would be such a good idea for you to go to the governor's mansion right now."

"Why not? It might give more validity to our story if we simply act normal."

"Story?" She glanced around as if someone might hear her. "This isn't a *story* we made up to cover some clandestine affair."

"I know."

Jasmine swallowed. How much she had wanted him to kiss her last night. "I mean, the fact that we are strictly friends is the truth."

"The whole truth," he agreed.

"And nothing but the truth," she finished, only to face another expanse of silence.

"Let's pray no one finds out I drove you home last night," he said finally, voicing her own uncomfortable thoughts.

"Too late," she said. "A reporter already told me he talked to the guard at my complex."

"Then the guard can confirm I only dropped you off."

"Somehow I don't think that clarification will make its way into the newspaper," she offered dryly, panic stabbing her anew. How had her life gone from smooth sailing to hurricane-tossed in less than twenty-four hours?

"Well, I told the mob that was here this morning in no uncertain terms that we were just friends."

"Thank you," she said, feeling awkward again. "I'll be attending a rally with the governor tonight, so maybe this whole thing will blow over soon."

"Sure," Ladden said. "It'll blow over in no time."

Jasmine studied her pink nails and forced innocence into her tone. "Ladden, this friend of yours . . . what made him think that you were, um, *crazy* about me?"

She detected an immediate change in his demeanor. Sexual energy crackled over the lines. She could picture him standing, his broad-shouldered frame dwarfing most of the items around him. Just when she decided her question would have been better left unasked, his warm voice came over the line.

"Probably the fact that I *am* crazy about you."

Pleasure and panic swelled in her chest, both vying for control. "Ladden—"

"I've got something to tell you," he cut in, "and it's going to sound pretty weird." He inhaled and exhaled noisily.

"What?" she asked, her heart thudding in anticipation.

"Jasmine," he said, his voice a hoarse whisper, "do you believe in magic?"

EIGHT

Ladden regretted the words as soon as they left his mouth. The strange events of the last few hours had been swirling in his head, and he'd felt a sudden impulse to share them with Jasmine. Only now he felt like a fool. How could he tell her about a genie granting him three wishes when two minutes ago, he hadn't believed it himself? She'd think he was a nut for sure.

"Ladden?"

"Uh, listen, Jasmine," he said, scrambling for words, "I need to go."

"But what were you going to say about magic?"

"I have a customer."

"I thought you were closed today."

"I'll call you."

"To let me know about the rug?"

"Uh, sure."

"Okay, but . . . are you all right?"

Ladden conjured up a forced laugh. "Never better. I'll talk to you later." He hung up with a hand that shook so badly he missed the handset cradle. Pulling himself to his feet, he noted with relief that at least the crowd at the front door had dissipated. He raised the blinds slowly, his mind spinning. He had to find the old man with the turban and satisfy himself that all the odd occurrences had reasonable explanations. "I'll be laughing about this tomorrow," he promised himself. Nodding with renewed confidence, he turned around—only to find the rug, rolled and on end, leaning against the frame of the door that connected the storeroom and showroom.

"How the hell . . . ?" Either he was losing his mind, or the rug was moving around of its own volition. Advancing toward the rug cautiously, he noticed a single monarch butterfly perched on top, its wings flapping silently.

Moving in a slow semicircle around the rug, he watched for any sign of movement. His eyes burned. "Okay, you, you . . . *thing*," he said, shaking his finger in warning, "you'd better stay put until the lady comes to tell me how much you're worth. If you move again, I swear I'll strap you down—"

"Ladden?"

He spun around to see Mrs. Pickney standing just inside the front entrance. "Who are you talking to?"

A hot flush climbed his neck as he straightened. "No one," he said, with a nervous laugh. "Just talking to myself. I didn't hear the bell."

"What a lovely rug," she exclaimed, walking over and fingering a corner of the carpet. The spooked butterfly floated toward the ceiling.

"Yes, it seems to be a favorite," Ladden said.

"I can see why," she murmured, smoothing her hand over a small section of pile. "It feels . . . special." A bewildered smile lit her face. "I've never seen anything like it."

Ladden pursed his lips in thought. Giving the rug to Mrs. Pickney seemed like a small token considering she was deeding him her entire store— and it would prevent the carpet from ending up in the bedroom of Trey McDonald. The thought of Jasmine digging her bare toes into the rug as she rolled out of the other man's bed rankled him beyond what he could bear. "It's yours if you want it, Mrs. Pickney."

The rug fell to the floor with a whoosh and a loud thud, startling them both and sending a cloud of dust billowing around their knees.

"Mine?" she asked, coughing and waving her hand to clear the air. "That's kind of you, son, but I'll be moving to my sister's soon and I won't have room." She grinned. "I got my permit for going out of business. Since my inventory is low anyway, I'll probably be cleaned out within a week or two."

"Mrs. Pickney, are you sure—"

"Yes," she said emphatically.

"I'll miss you."

She angled her white head at him. "I have a feeling you'll be too occupied with another woman to miss me. I heard about your billboards on the radio. I had no idea you were serious about anyone."

"Neither did I," he said miserably.

Her eyes twinkled. "Love sneaks up on you, doesn't it?"

He glanced back at the rug and frowned. "You could say I'm almost afraid to turn my back."

"Is it the young lady with the dark ponytail?"

Ladden winced. "Has it been that obvious?"

"No." She laughed. "It was a lucky guess. I've seen her come in and out of here quite a bit. I've often thought you'd make a nice couple."

"Thanks, but right now she and the governor make a nice couple."

"She dates Governor McDonald?"

"The one and only."

She dismissed the most powerful man in the state with a wave of a veined hand. "You're much more handsome."

"You're prejudiced, and besides, he's so rich, he can buy any face he wants."

"So? Women don't want money, Ladden." She lowered her voice. "Women want magic."

Ladden blinked. "M-magic?"

A faraway look came over her face. "You know, that *zing* you feel when you make eye contact across a room."

"Zing?"

She swept her arms above her head. "The fairy dust that falls around your shoulders when you dance."

"Fairy dust?"

She wiggled her wrinkled fingers in the air. "The fireworks that go off when you kiss."

"Fireworks?"

"I may be old," she said with a mischievous smile, "but I remember zing, fairy dust, and fireworks. Take my word for it, my dear . . . women want magic." With a fluttery wave, she was gone.

"Magic," he mumbled, turning back to the rug just as it began to unroll. The carpet gained momentum over the uneven wood floor and unfurled at the toe of his work boots with a snap of fringe. A flurry of butterflies materialized and hovered above the richly colored pile. Ladden looked heavenward and counted to ten. Then he calmly walked to the front door, stepped outside, and locked the door behind him.

During the short walk to the homeless shelter, Ladden recited the presidents' names, the states and their capitals, and as much of the periodic chart as he could recall to keep his mind occupied with thoughts other than a migratory carpet and personalized newspaper headlines. An old metal desk sat just inside the entrance to the shelter, manned by a stoop-shouldered fellow who glanced up at Ladden with a smile.

"Welcome. May I help you?"

Ladden twisted his hat in his hands. "I'm looking for a man I believe is staying here."

"Is he a relative?" the man asked, opening a ragged spiral notebook.

"No, just an acquaintance."

"Name?"

"I don't know. He's an older gentleman, wears some kind of white sarong"—Ladden gestured vaguely with his arms—"and a black turban."

The man's brow furrowed. "We have lots of turbans, but no sarongs. Are you sure he's staying here?"

"I dropped him off this morning."

"What time?"

"Around ten o'clock."

After running his finger down a log, the man shook his head. "Only three people signed in this morning, and I know all of them—no turbans. Sorry, pal."

Ladden thanked him, dropped a five dollar bill in the donation bucket, then looked around for the nearest travel agency that accepted major credit cards. He was feeling a bit impulsive, and a vacation was sounding better and better.

"Greetings, Master."

At the sound of the old man's voice, Ladden wheeled around. He was standing an arm's length away.

He inclined his turbaned head. The sarong was gone, replaced by clothing that resembled gray pajamas.

"Please don't call me Master. I'm Ladden."

"Yes, Master. You did not have to travel. A simple call would have summoned me."

Pursing his lips, Ladden asked, "What's your name?"

The man's face wrinkled into a deep frown. "Name?"

Did he have amnesia? Alzheimer's? "You don't remember your name?"

The man spread his arms wide. "I am only Genie, Master."

"Genie?"

"Yes, Master."

"How about just Gene?"

"I do not object."

"Okay, Gene, I need to talk to you about a couple of things. Let's grab a cup of coffee."

The man nodded and followed him at an embarrassingly subservient distance to a donut shop a few doors down. Ladden ordered them strong coffee, which Gene sipped tentatively, winced, then sipped again.

"Gene, do you remember the first time we met?"

"Of course, like it was yesterday."

"It *was* yesterday." Ladden tapped his fingers on the brown Formica tabletop. "My insurance company doesn't believe my claim that there was an earthquake, and I need for you to sign an affidavit that you witnessed it."

His brow creased. "An affi—?"

"A paper that says you were in my store during the earthquake."

"This word *earthquake*, what is it?"

Sighing, Ladden gulped the dark liquid in his cup. "Where the ground moves and destroys things, like that day in my store."

"Ah, I apologize for disturbing your things. So much pressure built up in the lamp."

"The lamp?"

"My home for the last few centuries."

Ladden took another swallow, then repeated, "Your home for the last few centuries?"

"Yes," the man said matter-of-factly. "My last master was an evil man. When I could not provide as much wealth as he desired, he instructed a wizard to banish me to the lamp." He grinned his gap-toothed grin. "For freeing me, my gift is to grant you three wishes. I have already granted wishes one and two."

Sweat gathered around Ladden's hairline. "Jog my memory. What were wishes one and two?"

"Why the market space next to yours, of course. And the message to your princess." Gene shrugged his thin shoulders. "I did not understand the term *crazy*, but I simply used your words, Master."

The hair rose on the back of Ladden's neck as he remembered the words he had spoken aloud in the cab of his truck . . . alone. Mrs. Pickney's decision to deed him her storefront was undoubtedly

a coincidence, but the message on the billboards . . .

"How did you know what my words were?"

"You spoke them aloud."

"But I was in my truck."

"I was with you."

Ladden's shoulders sagged in relief. The senile
man had probably crept into the back of his truck
to sleep and had overheard his comment about Jasmine. He nearly laughed aloud—the man almost
had him believing he was some kind of supernatu-
ral being. "You should have checked with me before you bought those billboards. They cost you a
lot of money."

Gene shook his head. "It is only paper—I print
great quantities."

*Great, he's not rich—he's a counterfeiter. They'll be
coming after me to collect—or imprison.*

Sure enough, the man reached into his pants
pocket and withdrew a thick stack of crisp one
hundred dollar bills. "Do you want money?"

"No!" Ladden held up his hand. "And put that
away, unless you want to get mugged."

"Mugged?"

"Robbed."

"Ah, thieves. My carpet and I used to give
them chase in the marketplace."

Ladden swallowed. "C-carpet?"

Nodding, Gene said, "He was a good friend in
the olden times—not in this United States of

America, but in another land, where it is much warmer."

"This rug . . . what does it look like?"

He squinted. "The color of berries, black around the edge." The old man shrugged. "That is all I remember. It has been a long time."

"Does it have fringe?"

His eyes bugged and he lurched forward. "Yes! Have you seen this carpet?"

Ladden gripped his coffee cup hard. "There is a rug of that description at my antique store."

"Where did you purchase it?"

"At the same auction I bought the lamp you referred to earlier."

A glow bathed the man's wrinkled face and his eyes shone. "My friend watched over me all these years."

With one quick motion, Ladden tossed down the last of the coffee. The story the man told was just too preposterous to believe. The old man must have seen the rug when he'd stolen the stationery envelope, and now seized the opportunity to embellish his fantasy with another detail . . . or perhaps the unstable man simply wanted to get his hands on the carpet and had fabricated the entire story.

"I am glad you have the carpet, Master," Gene said. "It is proper."

"I happen to agree, since I paid for it."

"Has your princess seen the carpet?"

"Jasmine? Yes, she's seen it."

Gene winked at him. "Do not worry. The carpet will help you gain favor with your lady."

Increasingly impatient with the man's rambling, Ladden tossed a couple of bills on the table. "Do you remember enough about the earthqua—I mean, the ground shaking, that you could tell someone else about it?"

The man nodded. "I will try, Master."

"Good. Let's go." He led the man toward the door. "And please don't call me Master."

"Yes, Master."

Two hours later, with a raging headache and heavy steps, Ladden unlocked the front door of his business. The old man had been worse than useless during their visit to Saul Tydwell's office. Even with much prompting from Ladden, his story had sounded sketchy, and his constant references to Ladden as Master on top of his ancient-sounding dialect had left Saul's face frozen in a mask of skepticism.

Ladden rummaged behind the big counter until he found a bottle of painkiller that hadn't expired. After swallowing two tablets with no water, he leaned on the counter and watched a butterfly explore a section of the smooth surface. He didn't dare look at the rug. He didn't even want to think about it. Besides, if he were going to reopen for business tomorrow, he needed to finish cleaning.

He grabbed the broom just as the phone rang. He was grateful for the distraction. "Hello?"

"Ladden, this is Betsy. I need your help."

At the sound of his housecleaner's voice, he relaxed slightly. "Is something wrong at my place?"

"No—although you really should hang some curtains in your bedroom." She lowered her voice to a teasing purr. "You never know when you might need some privacy."

Knowing the fiery Betsy was probably arched in some beguiling pose, he smirked. "Don't tell me that's what you need help with."

She laughed merrily. "Someday soon, I hope. For now, I need to borrow your furniture and your back."

"Got a catering gig tonight?"

"Right."

"And you need folding chairs?"

"Only fifty or so. I just found out I'll be serving on a patio and they expect me to provide the seating."

He smiled, eager to help a friend, glad that, for the first time today, something was within his control. "Fifty folding chairs, coming right up."

"Why don't you throw on a jacket and stick around till the party's over? We'll have fun and it'll save you a trip back."

Why not? He certainly didn't have anything else planned. "Sure. When and where?"

"Seven-thirty, the Shoalt Hotel."

"I'll meet you there."

NINE

Jasmine took a deep breath as she stepped from her car. After handing her key to the parking valet, she smoothed a hand over the skirt of the red crepe dress. Her nerves had been jangled all day, set on edge by her morning conversation with Ladden and frazzled further from ducking phone calls and checking her rearview mirror for reporters.

She'd managed to shake a news van that followed her when she left a deli at lunch. Her new client had hinted at the billboard controversy all day, but Jasmine had simply provided polite, evasive answers. Thankfully, when she drove home she noticed the billboards had been restored to their previous advertisements, predominantly Trey's. And when she arrived at her condo, there were no cameras in sight.

Still, she felt prickly and skittish as she entered

the grand lobby of the Shoalt Hotel. She told herself that, under the circumstances, it was perfectly
natural that Ladden Sanderson had been on her
mind all day . . . perfectly natural that she could
recall how well he filled his soft work shirt . . . or
how his eyes lit up when he smiled . . . or how
the corner of his mouth jumped when he teased
her.

"Good evening, Ms. Crowne." Joseph Elam,
administrative assistant to the governor, surveyed
her from head to toe and pursed his thin lips in
what appeared to be resignation.

"Hello, Mr. Elam."

He briefly indicated a large man standing a step
behind him. "This is Duncan."

She started to greet Duncan, but Mr. Elam cut
her off, sweeping his arm to the right. "Governor
McDonald will be glad to know you've arrived,"
he said in a voice that indicated he and the governor were not of like mind on the issue.

She realized with a sinking heart that after the
day's events, Elam had labeled her a liability to the
governor at this critical point in his campaign . . .
a distressing thought since she was so eager for
Trey to achieve his dreams. Another term as governor, then on to the Senate, then who only knew?
And although Trey hadn't proposed, he'd hinted
often enough that if she were so inclined, she
would be an asset to his political career. But
now . . .

Jasmine allowed herself to be steered through

the milling crowd, nodding to familiar faces, fairly trotting to keep up with Mr. Elam's pace. His eyes darted in all directions and he kept one arm half-curled a few inches from her waist, as if he intended to keep everyone away from her—or keep *her* away from everyone.

They moved past a ballroom where a jazz band played and threaded their way through several smaller rooms, each of which boasted a different theme with corresponding decorations and food. Heads turned her way and she noticed lingering glances and knowing smirks. She lifted her chin a little higher and painted on a bright smile, but inside she trembled—not out of fear of what people might be saying about her and Ladden Sanderson, but because of the guilt nibbling at her stomach. No matter how much she wanted it not to be true, even here in the company of the city's most powerful professionals she felt an inexplicable connection to and an undeniable longing for the quiet man who ran the antiques store on Pacific Street.

"There you are, my dear." Trey's deep voice broke into her thoughts, bringing her surroundings into focus. The governor looked regal in a dark suit, holding court in a room decorated with an Oriental flair, beneath elaborate paper dragons streaming across the ceiling. With clean-cut boyish looks and just the right amount of gray at his fair temples, he was a striking man. His dazzling smile appeared to be only for her as he turned away from a group of suited constituents. "You look beautiful, as always," he whispered before lowering a kiss to her cheek. Immediately, flashbulbs exploded around them.

Jasmine blinked and glanced over her shoulder—directly into more flashes. A knot of photographers loitered near the governor, pouncing without delay when she arrived.

"Ms. Crowne, is it true your car was towed yesterday for a parking violation?"

"Yes," she admitted and lifted her shoulders in a slow shrug. "I thought the parking meter had time left on it—it didn't. My mistake, and I paid for it."

"And is it true, Ms. Crowne, that a junk dealer named Ladden Sanderson drove you to your condo last night?"

She felt Trey stiffen, but she knew he wouldn't say anything in front of the cameras. "Yes, I had just left from making a purchase at Mr. Sanderson's *antiques store* when I discovered my car had been towed."

"Ms. Crowne, I have a witness who says you were seen with Mr. Sanderson last night at a bar called"—the man referred to his notes— "Tabby's."

A slow flush climbed her neck. "I was told I could find a phone at Tabby's, which is a family restaurant. Mr. Sanderson's family owns the establishment, and he happened to be there when I asked for a telephone."

"Do you frequent that bar, ma'am?"

"No, it was the first time I'd ever been there. Like I said, someone told me I could use the phone."

"And Mr. Sanderson just happened to be there?"

"That's correct."

"And he offered to drive you home?"

"Yes."

"And you accepted?"

She bit her tongue, fighting to control her rising anger. "Yes."

"Did he go in?"

A murmur traveled the crowd and Trey made a move to speak, but she silenced him with a nudge. "That, sir, is absolutely none of your business," she said evenly. "But since you'll print some half-truth if I don't respond, no, Mr. Sanderson did not come in."

"Governor McDonald, would you and Ms. Crowne care to comment about the billboards linking her romantically to Ladden Sanderson?"

Trey squeezed her against him and gave the reporter a cajoling smile. "Although I can clearly see why Ms. Crowne would attract her share of admirers, the signs were just a practical joke. Lighten up, folks."

"Ms. Crowne?"

She smiled broadly into the sea of onlookers, her heart thumping in her chest. "I think the governor summed up the situation."

"So you and Mr. Ladden are simply friends?"

"Business acquaintances," she corrected, distracted briefly by someone walking outside the window across the room. The man's head and shoulders were obscured by whatever he was carrying, but for some reason, the way he moved reminded her of Ladden. She glanced back to the audience and leaned closer to Trey, chiding herself. On the arm of the governor, no less, and she was thinking about another man!

"Governor McDonald, if you win the election, will the mansion remain a bachelor pad?"

Jasmine felt her cheeks grow even warmer as Trey chuckled and addressed the man. "Stan, if I ever decide to get married, I'm sure you'll know about it before I will."

The crowd laughed in appreciation. As always when they were in public, she stood in awe of Trey. He handled everyone so smoothly and with such confidence. And although he had assured her she would become more comfortable in the public eye as time passed, she had to admit that right now the *idea* of attending functions at the side of the most influential man in the state was far more appealing than actually *doing* it. In fact, her head was definitely starting to hurt, and wearing new high heels was proving to be a poor decision. She needed an aspirin and a Band-Aid.

Thankfully, another reporter asked a question that diverted attention from her to the more sobering subject of the drop in the governor's popularity in recent polls. Joseph Elam stepped in to point out that a Los Angeles paper had conducted an extensive survey that proved lobbyists supported the opponent, but the public supported Governor McDonald. "If every registered voter in California goes to the polls and votes their conscience, Governor McDonald will win by a landslide," Elam insisted. "But stay home, and you'll watch the governor's office be handed over to special interest groups."

"I think he wants my job," Trey whispered in her ear, causing her to smile.

"I think I'll mingle," she whispered back, and he gently released her.

"You look a little pale," he said, his brow wrinkling. "Are you feeling all right?"

"It's been quite a day," she said with as much cheer as possible. "I just need some air."

"I'll cover for you," he said with a wink. "But don't forget about me."

"Don't worry," she said, escaping in the direction of the patio. Appropriately, the theme outside resembled a luau, with tropical plants and servers wearing brightly colored shirts. Jasmine smiled at the scene. The pretty caterer, in her snug outfit, had attracted the attention of two state representatives.

Amid the wonderful-smelling food and the island music drifting on the balmy air, she tried to immerse herself in the festive mood. She spoke to a few acquaintances, deftly dodging their questions about the billboards. One tipsy woman commented on how ruggedly handsome the antiques dealer appeared in a clip on the news, and could Jasmine steer him her way since she was currently occupied with the governor?

The painful blister developing on her heel suddenly seemed unbearable, and she was grateful for the honest excuse to make her getaway.

A turbaned waiter from the Middle Eastern room walked by, his arms laden with a tray of exotic food. "Excuse me, sir," Jasmine said, touching his arm.

"Yes?" the man asked, offering a gap-toothed smile.

A chord of memory chimed in the back of her mind, but she couldn't place the man. "Could you direct me to the nearest ladies' room?"

He nodded. "Beyond those trees, you will find what you are looking for."

"Thank you." She turned and walked slowly around the patio, favoring her throbbing foot, cursing her vanity. However, once she made her way down a sloping footpath, her spirits lifted at the visual treat that lay before her.

A long, curving pool cast an aqua glow in the darkness, supplemented by floating candles. All poolside chairs had been removed, and the area appeared completely deserted, which seemed a shame. Away from the towering brightness of the hotel, the millions of stars twinkling above seemed close enough to pluck if she stood on tiptoe.

"A magical night," she whispered, then sighed

as she remembered Ladden's abandoned question. *"Jasmine, do you believe in magic?"*

Did she? When she was a child, she had often gazed out of her tiny bedroom window and wished on every shooting star, wished to be whisked far, far away. Yet it hadn't been magic that had delivered her into a world of opportunity—it had been sheer determination, a legal name change, and privately renouncing her only relative: her angry father.

She laughed, a soft, hollow sound. The move from Glenhayden didn't represent a great distance in miles, but comparing her life now to the one she'd left behind, she might as well be far, far away. Jasmine looked up to see a falling star shooting across the heavens, flashing, then petering out like a spent sparkler. She smiled. Perhaps magic had played a part in her life after all.

Shaking her head to clear her musings, she limped toward the changing rooms at the far end of the pool area and tugged on the door marked Women. The latch refused to budge, despite her best efforts and a futile pounding of her fist. Frustrated, she glanced at the door marked Men. It opened easily. She stuck her head inside and listened for sounds of activity, but only silence greeted her. A first aid kit hanging on the wall inside the door clinched her decision. She would only be a moment . . .

Ladden wiped down the last chair and tossed the soiled cloth in a crate in the back of his delivery truck. Slowly he swung to the ground and reached back to ease the last stack of chairs to his shoulder. Leveraging the weight with his legs as much as possible, he exhaled and wished he'd thought to bring a towel to protect his best white dress shirt. Oh, well, maybe his jacket would hide the worst of the smudges from the dozens of chairs he'd delivered to the patio. Not that the rest of his outfit mattered since Betsy had begged him to don a horrible Hawaiian print tie in keeping with the luau theme—although he *had* drawn the line at wearing a plastic lei.

The long, narrow path between the service parking lot and the patio smacked of pisspoor planning on the part of some architect, he thought irritably as he shuffled his way toward the music and bright lights. Once he arrived, Betsy abandoned her post behind the chicken and fruit kabob station to help him situate the chairs around the perimeter of the crowded brick patio.

"Thanks," she whispered, her face filled with anxiety. Her curly red hair sprang around her face, wet with perspiration and humidity. Seductively tucked into a long Hawaiian print skirt and matching halter top, Betsy looked like a slightly wilted flower.

"Hey, relax," he said with a wink. "You're doing great—the food's a big hit."

"Think so?" she asked, glancing around.

"Frank called me at the last minute to fill in for him. If I do a good job maybe he'll call again."

Ladden twisted to take in their brightly lit backdrop. "The entire hotel is hopping. Who's giving this party?"

Betsy shrugged. "Somebody rich, I suppose. All I know is Frank's paying me cash." She swiped at his shoulder. "Oh, your shirt is a mess. I'm sorry."

He waved off her concern. "Don't worry about it—but I think I'll duck into the men's room for a little repair. Is there anything else I can do?"

"I might need you to find the ice man when you get back."

"Sure thing." He craned his neck, looking for a rest room sign.

"Ladden."

He turned back, his eyebrows raised.

"You're the best." Betsy's eyes shone with gratitude and affection.

Ladden swallowed and shifted nervously. Why couldn't he simply fall for Betsy? After all, she was pretty and sweet. It was high time he got the silly notion of Jasmine Crowne out of his head. He gave her a fond smile. "Thanks, Betsy. I'll be right back."

He stopped to retrieve his dark suit jacket from a shelf under one of the skirted tables. The pungent smell of warm chlorine led him across a concrete footpath, away from the crowd, to a large kidney-shaped pool dotted with floating candles.

A dimly lit changing house sat at the opposite end, and he headed toward the men's side, already rolling up his sleeves. Whistling under his breath, he pushed open the heavy wood door and stepped into the large bathroom, the soles of his stiff shoes scraping on the terra-cotta-tiled floor.

A gasp and a movement stopped him in his tracks and he nearly choked in surprise. "Jasmine?"

Standing crookedly beside a padded bench in an area surrounded by lockers, she clutched one black high-heeled shoe to her chest. "Ladden?"

He simply stared at her for several seconds, then his words tumbled out around hers: "What—"

"—are you—"

"—doing here?"

The pinkish overhead bulbs caught the highlights in her upswept hair and bathed her skin with a sunkissed glow. Desire flooded his body and he fought to maintain control. She was stunning, even wearing a puzzled expression.

"Didn't you imagine I would be attending a political rally for Governor McDonald?"

Incredulous, he raked his hand through his hair. "I'm here helping a friend. I had no idea this party was for the governor." He glanced around the room. "But what are you doing *here?*"

She held up a small adhesive bandage. "A blister. I couldn't get inside the ladies' room."

Their compromising situation struck him full

force and he began a slow retreat. "Oh, hell—the media will fry us if anyone sees us." He held up his hand. "I'll go out first. Wait ten minutes, and if you don't hear anything, the coast is clear."

"Okay," she agreed, her eyes wide. "Good-bye."

His heart slammed against his ribs so hard, the beat echoed deep in his ears. When he felt the door at his back, he turned and yanked the latch. When the door refused to budge, he put more muscle behind it. Only after he set aside his jacket, used both hands, and still the door wouldn't give did panic begin to mushroom in his chest.

"What's wrong?" she asked, her voice squeaky.

"The door's stuck."

"Well, unstick it!"

"I'm trying." He braced his foot against the frame and pulled on the rusty latch with all his might. After jiggling the knob side to side, he said, "I think it's locked."

"Locked!" she shrieked. "How could the door be locked?"

Ladden exhaled in frustration and looked over his shoulder. "I don't know. Didn't you say you couldn't get inside the women's rest room?"

Her eyes closed briefly. "Yes."

"Maybe the latches are faulty."

"Oh, my God." She dropped her shoe and covered her mouth with her hands.

"Okay, don't panic," he said, more for his benefit than for Jasmine's. "Maybe there's another way out." He walked into the locker area and studied the high windows around the perimeter of the room. After testing a small table for sturdiness, he climbed up and succeeded in cranking open a window—six inches.

"I can't even get my hand out to wave a flag for help," he said.

"We can't attract attention, anyway." Her voice trembled. "You and I locked in a bathroom together—this would look very, very bad." She sank heavily onto the faded cushions of a floral couch and put her head in her hands. "What are we going to do?"

"Someone will find us."

"But we can't be found!" Jasmine rocked back and forth. She'd discarded the other shoe and sat with her stockinged feet on the tiled floor. "Half of Sacramento already thinks we're having an affair thanks to those billboards!"

"I know," he said miserably. "I'm sorry."

"The last thing Trey needs right now is a full-fledged scandal."

"I know," he repeated, walking over to her. "Believe me, I'm sorry."

She glanced up at him. "I don't suppose that well-intended friend of yours had anything to do with *this*."

Ladden pursed his lips—then shook his head. "Gene wouldn't go that far."

"Gene?"

He lowered himself to the bench, a good distance from where she sat. "This old homeless guy who says"—he laughed—"who says he lived in the copper lamp you bought and is going to grant me three wishes for releasing him from bondage."

A strange smile curved her mouth. "You mean, this guy thinks he's magic?"

"Something like that." He felt his ears growing hot.

"How on earth did you meet this strange person?"

"Remember the day of the earthquake tremor?"

"Yes."

"He must have been walking by my store when it happened because when things settled down, I found him sitting in front of the counter."

"That's odd."

"The next thing I know he's calling me Master and ranting about granting me three wishes."

She laughed, a tinkling sound that stirred his blood. "He sounds like one for the books."

"Definitely."

"Well," she said in a teasing voice, "did you make your wishes?"

Ladden debated for a moment whether to reveal the rest of the story, the bizarre coincidences, the weird goings-on with the carpet. Hell, for all she knew, he could have followed her here tonight and planned this entire episode.

"Ladden," she said more softly, with a slight catch in her voice, "did you make your wishes?"

TEN

Jasmine stared at the dark-haired man next to her, her throat dry. Of course, the very concept of wishes being granted was preposterous, but his hesitation spoke volumes.

He exhaled noisily, puffing out his smooth cheeks, then met her gaze. "I, um . . . I did inadvertently say, um, a couple of things that . . . happened."

The hair stood up on her arms. "Wh-what things?"

After an awkward laugh, he said, "Well, I was a little frustrated with the tremor damage yesterday, and my place is getting so crowded . . . I sort of wished aloud that my neighbor would retire and give me *her* storefront."

"And?"

"And this morning she . . . she announced

she was going to retire and wanted to give me her storefront."

The story sounded too fantastic. "Had she ever hinted at doing such a thing?"

Ladden shook his head. "No. We've been friends for years, and I kind of helped her with the repairs and stuff after her husband died, but I never expected—or dreamed—something like this would happen. It was just a crazy statement, something off the top of my head."

"Does she have children?"

"No."

"Then it's possible she meant to give you the space all along and simply hadn't mentioned it."

"That's what I thought . . . at first."

"And then?"

He stood and turned his back to her, offering a nice view of his physique. His shoulders filled the dress shirt impressively, then gave way to a narrow waist and trim hips enclosed in dark slacks. She'd never seen him wear anything other than jeans, and the transformation was astonishing. With a few inches off his longish hair, he could blend in easily inside any corporate boardroom—although his exceptional shoulders might betray the fact that he didn't sit behind a desk all day.

Ladden cleared his throat and said quickly, "After I dropped you off last night, I sort of wished aloud that you could see how crazy I was . . . am . . . about you."

Her skin tingled with desire at his admission. "You said this when you were driving home?"

"Yeah."

Her mouth fell open slightly. "And the billboards . . ."

He nodded slowly.

She laughed nervously and rose to her feet. "But there's nothing magic about arranging for billboard space—I mean, if this crazy old man did it, he must have overheard you say something about"—she felt a flush warm her neck—"me."

"I thought perhaps he had crawled in the back of the truck without me realizing it and overheard me, but it seems like a stretch."

"Oh, and the alternative isn't a stretch?"

"Yes, but there's more."

"More?"

"Last night before you dropped in at Tabby's, the bartender gave me a note from someone who fit this fellow Gene's description."

"That was the note your uncle was teasing you about?"

He smirked. "Right."

"What did it say?"

After a slight hesitation, he said, "It said, 'A wise first wish, Master.'"

She shrugged. "There's nothing magic about a handwritten note."

"How about a customized newspaper headline?"

"What?"

"This morning when I opened my paper, the entire front page read, 'A Wise Second Wish, Master.'"

A laugh of disbelief bubbled out of her throat. "Ladden, that's impossible. Did you keep the newspaper?"

He pressed his lips together, then dropped his gaze and said in a low voice, "The wind scattered the paper and I couldn't find the front page."

"What about the note?"

"I found it this morning. You scribbled your tag number on the back."

"I remember."

He lifted his gaze once again. "But the other side was completely blank."

Jasmine shook her head slowly. "This is starting to spook me. Ladden, if I didn't know better—"

"You'd think I was insane," he finished for her. He lifted his hands. "Hell, maybe I am."

Searching his face, she asked, "Did you call the sign company? Someone had to cover all that expense."

Nodding, he said, "They received a stationery envelope with my store's letterhead full of new one-hundred-dollar bills."

She swallowed hard. "Maybe he stole an envelope."

"Maybe."

"Maybe he's rich and eccentric."

Ladden gave her a wry smile. "He said he

printed his own money and showed me a stack of bills that looked too new to be real, so I doubt that he's rich, and I wonder how much trouble I'll be in if he paid for the billboards with counterfeit money."

"You have to go to the police."

He laughed and looked heavenward. "It'll be hard for me to run my business wearing a strait-jacket."

"But you have his name."

"Not really. He calls himself Genie, I call him Gene."

"Do you know where he lives?"

"He seems to simply show up—complete with turban."

Jasmine felt as if her body's functions had come to a screeching halt. Her heart stopped, her throat tightened, and the muscles in her legs gave way. She sank to the bench. "A turban? A b-black tur-ban?"

Ladden didn't even have to answer—the ex-pression on his face told her. He joined her on the bench, looking somewhat boneless himself. "Don't tell me you know him."

Vague recollections flooded her mind and she rubbed her temples. "Not really, but the night my car was towed, a street vendor wearing a black tur-ban directed me to your family's tavern to use the phone."

"It could be a different man."

"But the next morning when a cab arrived, I thought the man looked familiar."

Ladden dropped his head in his hands. "I'd forgotten that Gene told me he was with you when you saw the billboards."

"He's here."

His head snapped up. "Gene's here?"

"Now I'm sure it's the same man, but when I first saw him I assumed he was in costume."

"Did he talk to you?"

"Yes . . ." She felt the blood drain from her face. "I asked him for directions to the ladies' room and he sent me here." She staggered to her feet, backing away until the wall of metal lockers stopped her.

Ladden's face was anguished. "Jasmine, I know this looks bad, but I swear to you I didn't have anything to do with this."

And while her head screamed danger, something inside her knew by his pained expression that he was telling the truth—that he, too, was a victim of this lunatic matchmaker. She relaxed slightly and nodded, gulping for air. "Okay. I believe you. Do you think he locked us in?"

He sighed, glancing back toward the door. "It's possible, but . . ."

"But what?"

"How did he know I'd be coming here?"

"Did you tell anyone? Could he have been eavesdropping?"

He murmured, "I told Betsy on the patio, but I

walked down here within a few seconds of telling her."

Betsy? The red-haired woman in the sexy outfit? Considering the floral tie he wore, it seemed likely that the female caterer was the friend he'd mentioned he was helping. Suddenly, the thought of Ladden having a girlfriend rankled her.

"The timing doesn't seem right," he said. "Unless he gave you directions immediately after he overheard me."

Feeling sheepish, she shook her head. "I stopped to stargaze for a few minutes along the way. You would've arrived first." She smacked the locker behind her and the metallic clatter reverberated in the room. "There has to be a reasonable explanation."

"There's more," he said.

Jasmine laughed hysterically. "More?"

He nodded, shifting from foot to foot, his face reddening.

"What?"

"The rug you want."

"What about it?"

"It, um . . . it moves."

Now she'd heard everything. "It moves?"

Ladden's face flamed next to his white shirt. He loosened his tie and looked away. "Yeah."

"You mean it lies on the floor and vibrates?"

"Not exactly."

"Then what, exactly?"

"I hung it on the wall, it fell down."

Her shoulders sagged. "Is that all?"

"Then I put it on some trunks and it moved to a table, then to a doorway. I rolled it up and set it in a corner, and it moved to the showroom."

Incredulous, she asked, "You actually saw this rug levitate and move around?"

"No—I turned my back and the next thing I knew, the rug was somewhere other than where I left it."

"Okay, now you're scaring me," she said, holding up a hand and attempting a laugh.

"Gene said it was a magic carpet."

"We're back to Gene again?"

Pressing the heels of his hands into his temples, he said, "It sounds insane—I'm just telling you what I know."

She ticked off the situation on her fingers. "So far we have an old copper lamp, a mysterious earthquake, a man who claims to be a genie who is shadowing both of us, two so-called wishes that have been 'granted,' a disappearing note, a missing newspaper headline, and a flying carpet."

Ladden said nothing.

She cocked her head at him, her heart expanding. "Is this what you were leading up to this morning when you asked me if I believed in magic?"

He looked away and didn't answer for so long, she stepped toward him. "Ladden?"

"I wanted to tell someone," he said mournfully. "Forget it, Jasmine, if I had the money, I'd commit *myself.*"

Even as she tried to think of comforting words, Jasmine experienced a disturbing realization: she couldn't bear to see Ladden so unhappy. "Hey," she said, reaching around to touch his arm, "everyone feels crazy at one time or another." Muscle moved beneath her fingers and the soft cotton of his shirt as he turned toward her.

"I'm sorry you were dragged into this," he said quietly, his brown eyes serious. A shadow of whiskers darkened his jaw at this late hour, and he looked unbelievably handsome with his black hair curling around the stark white collar of his shirt. She couldn't pull her gaze from his.

"Looks like we'll be here for a while," she murmured, all too aware they were only an arm's length apart. A slow, sensual song was wafting from the intercom, echoing off the hard, flat surfaces in the small room.

"How's your blister?" he asked with a soft smile.

Jasmine blinked and dragged her gaze down to inspect her stockinged foot, wriggling it. "Fine, without shoes."

"Fine enough to dance?"

Surprised, she looked up, her breath catching in her throat.

"I'm a little rusty," he said quickly, "but I'll do my best not to tread on your bare toes."

She searched his eyes and saw warm affection

shining in their depths. She told herself she shouldn't—she couldn't—accept a dance from a man she knew had a crush on her, a crush that had somehow led to several strange events, which together now posed a threat to Trey's reelection. Yet even as she mentally reviewed the list of reasons to say no, she stepped closer and shyly lifted her left arm to his shoulder, then waited for him to clasp her right hand.

He smiled, then angled his body toward hers, gently taking her hand and sweeping her into a slow, sweet waltz. Yet even with the chaste distance between their bodies, Jasmine's skin burned where his hand curved around her waist and where his palm met hers. With perfect timing and a light touch, he led her around the close room in small circles.

"Where," she asked, "did you learn to dance?"

"In Aunt Silvie's kitchen," he said, "but watch your toes, because I can't talk and count at the same time."

She laughed and leaned into him involuntarily. Without missing a beat, he took up the slack and reduced the distance between them. "You look very nice," she said, and meant it.

"You," he said quietly, "are breathtaking. Unfortunately, I can't stare and count at the same time either."

Relaxing further into him, she told herself she shouldn't be having such a good time, but she didn't want it to end. Without warning, the waiter's words, which she hadn't given much thought to at the time, came back to her. *"Beyond those trees, you will find what you are looking for."*

Jasmine looked into Ladden's eyes, which were too honest to hide his desire for her. Her breasts grew taut and her thighs warmed in response. Had she? Had she found what she was looking for? Or was theirs simply a strong physical attraction, elevated by their odd circumstances and sudden proximity. The song faded to an end. Their bodies stilled, but they did not release one another.

Slowly, oh so slowly, Ladden lowered his head, his gaze riveted on her mouth. She had plenty of time to stop him with a movement or a protest, but Jasmine simply listened to her heart pound and wet her lips in preparation for his kiss.

With his mouth a whisper away from hers, he stopped, as if giving her a last chance to resist him, but she could not. Instead, she flicked out the tip of her tongue to invite him inside. With a groan, he captured her mouth fully and crushed her against his chest as if he were afraid she would escape. She opened her mouth to his tongue and moaned as he explored inside. He tasted of salt and mint, a tantalizing combination. His hands kneaded her back slowly and she sensed a restraint in his caresses that made her tremble.

Feeling tiny and pliable in the circle of his arms, Jasmine timidly snaked her hands around his neck. Her fingers skimmed over the knotty muscles beneath the cloth of his shirt. He raised his head and lifted her off the floor as he dipped his head lower to rain kisses along the length of her neck. His hands strumming her back ignited so many fires, Jasmine thought she would surely be consumed.

Ladden rasped her name against her neck and licked at the sensitive skin of her exposed collarbone. She rolled her shoulders and leaned her head back, arching in his arms, fully supported by him. Her skirt had shimmied up to expose the black garter belt holding up her thigh-high stockings. When his searching hand found bare skin, he groaned, then stiffened.

Immediately, she sensed his withdrawal. He lifted his head, his chest heaving, and lowered her to the floor as if she were a priceless, breakable object. "Jasmine," he whispered, his eyes large and apologetic, "I'm sorry. This isn't how it should be, how I want it to be."

Lowering her arms, she smoothed down the skirt of her dress, still reeling from the blow his body had delivered to her senses. "You're right, of course," she said shakily. "I don't know what came over me."

He smiled wryly, not attempting to hide the hard ridge of his erection. "*I* would have if we hadn't stopped when we did."

Grateful for his humor in such an awkward moment, she returned his smile.

"Thank you for the dance," he said, inclining his head.

Struggling to control her breathing, Jasmine checked her hair in the mirror and offered Ladden a tissue for the lipstick stains around his mouth, although she couldn't offer much help for the red smear on his collar. Like two high school kids making repairs before going home, they righted their clothing and hair. She drew on her lipstick with a shaky hand, trying to squash the panic that threatened to overwhelm her.

"Jasmine," he said quietly, squinting as he re-tied the horrid floral tie. "Will you go out with me?"

She caught his gaze in the mirror. "Out?"

"You know, maybe dinner and a movie?"

Inhaling deeply, she applied another layer of color to her lips, hoping to erase the lingering sensation of his mouth on hers. "Ladden, I think we have a more imminent problem here."

"Which is?"

She put down her lipstick and stared at him in the mirror. "How are we going to get out of here?"

Shrugging his big shoulders, he said, "I have no idea."

Unable to resist, she ventured, "You could use your third wish."

"My what?"

"Your third wish," she teased. "Don't you have one left?"

A mischievous light flared in his eyes, causing her pulse to kick up again. Moving behind her with animal grace, he lowered his mouth to her ear and whispered, "I *would* be ready for a straitjacket if I used my last wish to get away from you."

A loud knock on the door sent her heart to her throat. Ladden jumped as well, then waved her farther into the rest room as he approached the door.

"Ladden, are you in there?" Betsy's voice rang out.

She saw his shoulders drop in relief. "Betsy," he called, "the door locked behind me—I can't get out."

The woman's laughter reached Jasmine's ears, a bit brassy, but a welcome sound. "Are you alone in there?" she asked, her voice lilting. "Maybe I should come in."

Ladden glanced back to Jasmine and gestured frantically for her to hide. She weighed her choices, then jumped in a shower stall and pulled the curtain closed.

"Come on, Betsy, let me out," he yelled.

Jasmine heard rattling and thumping, then Ladden proclaimed in a loud voice, "Whew! It sure is nice to be out of this place. I think I'll prop open the door with a rock so no one else will get locked in."

"Why are you yelling?" the woman asked. "And what did you spill on your shirt?"

Their voices faded and Jasmine counted to one hundred, then scrambled out of her hiding place. She slapped a Band-Aid on her stocking over the blister, shoved her feet in her shoes, then peeked outside. Thankfully, the coast seemed clear. Heaving a sigh of relief, she made her escape and retraced her steps alongside the pool, which was still deserted. Her mind spun, replaying the fantastic tales he'd told her and their lapse, which had very nearly led to disaster. Right now she was sure of one thing—she could not allow herself to get emotionally attached to Ladden. She hadn't clawed her way out of Glenhayden and up the social ladder of Sacramento to marry an antiques dealer with a too-vivid imagination.

No, she decided, quickening her step, Ladden Sanderson didn't figure into her lifelong dreams. She had gone as far as the deep end of the pool when a powerful gust of wind swirled around her, ruffling the giant leaves of the tropical plants in the landscaping. Jasmine gathered the hem of her dress in one hand, and tried to hold her hair in place with the other. She stumbled sideways, then steadied herself mere inches from the edge. Her heart pumped adrenaline through her trembling body . . . she couldn't swim. Then a gust carrying the force of human hands knocked her off balance. Scrambling desperately for a foothold, Jasmine clawed the air in terror and screamed just before she plunged beneath the surface.

ELEVEN

Ladden positioned himself in a spot on the patio where he could watch for Jasmine's return as unobtrusively as possible. Betsy, having teased him mercilessly on the way back, was now perched next to the melting ice sculpture whose demise was undoubtedly being hastened by the scorching glances of the two men hanging on her every word.

He had a beer halfway to his mouth when a scream from the direction of the pool pierced the air. His brain processed the sound in a split second . . . Jasmine! With his heart in his throat, Ladden pushed through the crowd and hurdled over low tables. He pounded down the path leading to the pool, frantic, turning in all directions.

"Jasmine, where are you?" Then he saw a movement in the deep end of the shadowy pool. A flash of red confirmed his worst fear. "Noooooo!" he roared, going from motionless to a dead run in the space of a heartbeat, tearing off his jacket just before he dove off the edge and sliced the surface. Jasmine's eyes were closed and she floated virtually motionless, her dark hair like tentacles around her pale face.

Moving without rational thought, Ladden grabbed her waist and dragged her to the surface with two massive kicks. He threw back his head and gulped air, yelling for help as he hauled her limp body to the side. A gasping crowd had gathered and several people helped him lift her from the water. He heaved himself up over the edge of the pool and despite the fear that threatened to paralyze him, immediately began to administer mouth-to-mouth resuscitation, talking to her between transferring the breath from his lungs into hers.

"Jasmine. Wake up. Wake up and talk to me." He kept his emotion in check, barely. She needed him to be strong, to stay calm. "Come on, Jasmine, breathe, baby, breathe." When he shoved his ear to her mouth to listen for signs of recovery, he heard a weak gurgle in her throat. He jerked up and squeezed her hand. "Breathe, Jasmine, breathe." Her chest heaved and she sputtered, spewing water. Weak with relief, he turned her on her side to help expel the liquid, vaguely aware of the crowd applauding. "Stand back," he yelled. "Give her room!"

Within a few seconds, he heard a siren in the

distance. "You're okay," he whispered, smoothing her dark hair back from her colorless face.

"Ladden?" she gasped. "A freak wind . . . must have lost my balance."

"Shhh, don't talk, just try to relax and concentrate on breathing." Flashes of light exploded on all sides. Enraged, Ladden bellowed at the crowd and pulled down Jasmine's dress to cover her thighs.

"Let the governor through!" someone shouted, and he looked up in time to see McDonald burst through the crowd, his face a gray mask.

"Jasmine!" he yelled, kneeling by her and grasping her hand.

Immediately, Ladden pulled back, rising to his feet and testing his rubbery legs.

"What happened?" the governor asked.

"We heard a scream," a lady said.

"When we got here, she was floating in the deep end," someone else chimed in.

"This guy dove in and saved her," a man finished.

McDonald stood and extended his hand to Ladden. "Mister, you're a hero. I'm Governor McDonald and I am deeply in your debt. What's your name?"

After a few seconds' hesitation, Ladden said, "Sanderson."

The other man's brow crinkled slightly. "Sanderson, did you say?"

"That's right. Ladden Sanderson."

"It's that Sanderson guy," someone yelled, and more flashes went off.

The governor's lips formed a tight, hard line and he gripped Ladden's hand a little harder. He leaned forward and lowered his voice until Ladden could barely hear him. "If I find out you had anything to do with this, that you tried to hurt her—"

"I heard a scream, and I came running," Ladden cut in, tightening his own grip. "I delivered chairs for a caterer. I had no idea you or Ms. Crowne would be here."

"Right," McDonald snapped. "That must be one hell of a rug Jasmine is so determined to buy from you."

"Trey," Jasmine said. Some color had returned to her face and she slowly pushed herself up to a sitting position. Ladden nearly butted heads with McDonald when they both knelt to help her. But when the governor gave him a nasty look, Ladden backed off. After all, she had asked for the other man.

"Yes, darling," McDonald crooned.

"Mr. Sanderson is a good man and a good friend," she said, glancing toward Ladden, her eyes moist. "I simply lost my balance on those ridiculous shoes and fell into the pool." She wet her lips carefully. "I owe Mr. Sanderson my life."

McDonald glanced up, his eyes narrowed. "So, Mr. Sanderson, it was mere coincidence that you were in the right place at the right time?"

Ladden ground his teeth. "I suppose so."

"Then I must thank you," he said politely, but his eyes remained flat.

The paramedics arrived on the scene, checked Jasmine's vital signs, and pronounced her nearly fully recovered. Security succeeded in clearing the crowd, leaving only a knot of people closely associated with the hotel or with the governor, and Ladden. McDonald wanted Jasmine to go to the hospital, but she insisted she only needed rest and a hot shower.

"I'll drive you," Ladden said in unison with McDonald, which garnered him another glare from the governor.

Standing now and wrapped in one of the hotel's robes, her eyes darted back and forth between them. "I'll get a room here at the hotel, and I'll be fine."

"I'll walk with you," Ladden said in unison with McDonald. They traded glares again.

"Trey, would you excuse me and Mr. Sanderson for a moment? I'll be right there."

McDonald frowned, but nodded and moved out of earshot, although he stood behind Jasmine, within Ladden's line of vision.

Ignoring the other man, Ladden studied her eyes and drank in the contours of her pale face, his hands itching to pull her close. "Are you sure you're okay?" he breathed.

She smiled and nodded, but her eyes welled. "Thank you, Ladden."

He bit his tongue hard. "Jasmine, if you start

crying, I swear I'm going to scoop you up and carry you out of here, governor or no governor."

"I don't know what happened," she said. "I lost my balance, and I fell, and I can't swim—" She broke off in a choked voice.

Ladden sighed. "You're determined to make me do something McDonald will regret, aren't you?"

She shook her head and sniffed mightily.

"Better give me a smile since loverboy is getting nervous," he said lightly.

"I ruined your suit," she said miserably.

"It wasn't an Armani."

"Ladden, about this evening—"

"We'll talk about it some other time," he said. "You need rest."

She gave him a watery smile. "I'll call you tomorrow." Her chin went up. "Because I still want that rug."

Ladden glanced at McDonald, who looked like he was ready to charge. "For *his* bedroom, I think the price just went up. You'd better get going."

He watched as she walked away with McDonald, his heart twisting when the other man wrapped a possessive arm around her waist. He'd lost her for the night . . . but at least he hadn't lost her for good.

Turning to leave, he nearly walked into the massive Duncan, who offered him a tight smile. "Mr. Sanderson, the governor has asked me to follow you home and make sure you arrive safely.

And we need to have another little talk about Ms. Crowne."

"Our top news story this morning," the anchorwoman said, "is the near drowning that occurred last evening at the Shoalt Hotel during a political rally for Governor McDonald. The victim was none other than the governor's girlfriend, Jasmine Crowne, who reportedly cannot swim and fell into a pool by accident. It is not known if alcohol was a factor, but the story took an ironic twist when it was discovered that the man who pulled her from the water and resuscitated her is Ladden Sanderson, the same gentleman who only yesterday was linked romantically to Ms. Crowne by a bizarre message on several billboards on the bypass." The woman's mouth quirked. "Political analysts say this is yet another blow to Governor McDonald's image, and does not bode well for the upcoming election."

Cursing, Ladden turned off the television, then padded downstairs for his morning ritual of breakfast and paper on the porch. He hadn't slept well. He couldn't stop thinking about Jasmine . . . their dance, their kisses, the warmth of her body next to his . . . and the incredible terror he felt when he pulled her from the pool. God, how he'd wanted to be with her last night, just to watch over her.

The only good news, he decided when he

opened the paper, was that he didn't have a customized headline. The bad news was that the featured photograph showed him reviving Jasmine, which to the casual reader looked as if they were locked in an intimate embrace.

Both Mrs. Matthews and Mrs. Hanover traipsed over to try and squeeze any tidbit of gossip they could out of him, but he managed to gloss over the details and dismiss the media's assertion that Governor McDonald's campaign had stumbled because of his "friendship" with Jasmine.

He was glad to be reopening the store today, he decided as he pulled his truck into the alley. Customers would help keep his mind off Jasmine. The rug expert would be stopping by, he remembered, and he needed to start making plans for his new store space.

It came as no surprise to him that the rug was once again spread over the table he'd been holding for Jasmine. He saluted as he walked by, closed the door connecting the storeroom and showroom, then picked up the phone and arranged for another antiques dealer to deliver the table to the governor's mansion. The last thing he needed was another run-in with McDonald, especially after Duncan's none-too-subtle threats last night.

The morning passed quickly. Business was brisk, with new customers who were curious and old customers who stopped by for coffee and gossip. And he had a barrage of phone calls from family and friends who wanted just the gossip, hold the coffee. He had managed to put the other strange incidents of the last few days out of his mind until the bell rang and Marie Davies walked in with a smile and her magnifying glass to inspect the rug.

Ladden stepped from behind the counter, feeling suddenly nervous about letting someone else examine the carpet. "Hello, Ms. Davies."

"Hello, Ladden." She peered over her half-glasses. "You're quite the celebrity, I hear."

"Don't believe everything you read," he warned.

"I've worked with Ms. Crowne on several occasions—a lovely woman, I'm so glad she's all right."

"So am I. In fact, Ms. Crowne is the designer who wants to buy the rug."

"For an account of hers?"

"Something like that," he muttered.

"From your description of the carpet over the phone, I must admit, I'm very intrigued."

"Give me a moment to retrieve it," he said. "I, um, have trouble keeping up with it." He backed away with a smile and opened the door to the storeroom tentatively, his heart sinking when he saw the rug had once again scampered away. But this time he couldn't find it. He peered behind and under every piece of furniture, and after twenty minutes, he was ready to concede defeat.

"Is there a problem?" Ms. Davies poked her head through the doorway.

He shrugged sheepishly. "I can't find the carpet. I've been moving things around so much lately, I must have misplaced it."

"By chance, is that the rug?" Ms. Davies asked, her head tilted back.

Ladden followed her gaze and nearly swallowed his tongue. Indeed the rug was against the ceiling, a good thirty feet above their heads—and he had absolutely no idea how to retrieve it. "Um, n-no, that's not the rug," he lied. He tucked the note on which he'd scribbled the foreign markings from the lamp back into his pocket. "I must have packed it away and simply forgot. I don't want to take up any more of your time."

But she still stared at the ceiling. "How on earth did you get that carpet up there?"

"I-I didn't," he stammered. "I mean, it was already there."

"When you bought the place?"

He cleared his throat. "Uh-huh."

Her thin eyebrows rose. "You really should find a way to get it down. From here it looks Indian, and the markings are some of the most ancient I've seen." She nodded emphatically. "You could have a museum-quality piece up there."

"Thanks, Ms. Davies," he said, ushering her back into the showroom. "I apologize for the inconvenience."

"Call me when you find the rug," she said, "*and* when you get your hands on the carpet on the ceiling."

"Will do," he said, waving cheerfully, wondering what he'd tell Jasmine now about the rug she wanted for her boyfriend's boudoir. He scrubbed a hand over his face. "Where's a genie when you need one?"

"Greetings, Master," a familiar voice said behind him.

Ladden froze and turned slowly to see Gene, new pajamas, same turban. "Hey, Gene. You could give a person the creeps the way you pop in and out of places."

"Did you need something, Master?"

Ladden lowered his voice to a menacing level. "As a matter of fact, buddy, I have a bone to pick with you. Leave Jasmine alone. We compared notes last night after you lured us to the men's room and locked us in. You're a weirdo, and if I see you around here or around Jasmine again, I'm going to call the police and have you hauled off to a looney farm, got it?"

The man's thick gray eyebrows knitted. "You were not happy to be alone with your princess?"

Ladden felt like shaking the man. "Of course, but not when it's so, so . . . underhanded. What if she thinks I put you up to it? I'm lucky she's even speaking to me."

"Sometimes extreme measures are required." Gene grinned widely. "You saved her life, did you not?"

Frowning at the man's gleeful expression, Ladden answered warily. "Yes, but barely."

Gene scoffed. "I made sure you had plenty of time."

Ladden went completely still. "What are you saying?"

Another gap-toothed grin. "I arranged for Ms. Crowne to fall into the pool so you could save her life!"

"You *what?*"

"I knew she couldn't swim—"

Ladden cut off his words with a hand around his windpipe. *"You pushed her in?"* A red haze descended over his eyes and his stomach boiled. "She could have died because of you!"

"Master," the man sputtered in a strangled voice, "I knew . . . you would . . . save her . . . I cannot . . . take a life."

But Ladden only tightened his grip around the man's scrawny throat.

"Ladden, boy, what are you doing?" Ernie boomed behind him, then lunged between the men to break Ladden's death grip. Gene stumbled backward, coughing and gasping for air.

His uncle shook him by the shoulders. "You might have killed that man."

Seething, Ladden said, "I might still."

"Hush now," Ernie chided. "You have customers."

Gene straightened, his face sad and crumpled. "But Master, I only wanted you and your princess—"

"Shut up!" Ladden snapped. "Enough with the

Master and the princess garbage! I'm calling the police." He charged to the phone, but when he put the handset to his mouth and turned around, the old man was gone.

"Where did he go?" Ernie asked, turning in a full circle, craning his neck.

With a loud sigh, Ladden replaced the phone. "The man's a lunatic—he has a way of disappearing." He ran his hand through his hair, his nerves frayed.

"What did he do?"

"He's been harassing Jasmine, and as good as admitted he pushed her in the swimming pool last night."

"The paper said she fell."

"The paper also insinuated she might have been drunk."

"Was she?"

"No!" Ladden slumped against an old desk. "What a freaking mess!"

"Yeah . . . well, Ladden, I came to deliver bad news," Ernie said soberly.

Ladden straightened. "What?"

"The health department inspector just closed down Tabby's."

TWELVE

"So tell me about this Sanderson guy," Trey said casually.

Jasmine glanced up in surprise. Intent on the brunch menu, Trey appeared scrupulously uninterested, but she wasn't fooled. Her body temperature increased instantly. "What do you mean?"

"I mean," he said, closing the menu and setting it aside, "is there or isn't there something going on between the two of you?"

She didn't need this—not after lying awake all night, confused and restless, reliving Ladden's kiss a hundred times, wallowing in the feelings he'd evoked. "Trey, don't tell me you're starting to believe the newspapers."

"No—I know the closest thing to the truth in the papers is the comics. But"—he leaned forward—"why didn't you tell me he drove you home the other night?"

Just yesterday, she'd seen a segment on television about how to tell if someone is evading the truth. She concentrated on not doing any of those things. "Why didn't I tell you?" Oops—repeating the question was one of the signs. "Trey, election day is less than two weeks away. Why would I bother you with an insignificant detail about who dropped me off at my condo after my car was towed?" She manufactured a laugh—another telltale sign—then swallowed hard—yet another sign. "If I wanted to be clandestine about it, would I have ridden in a big old delivery truck with the name of his business written on the side?"

"Okay, okay, so I'm imagining things," he relented with a smile. "I guess I'm nervous about the wrap-up tour."

"You'll be great," she said with sincerity, touching his hand. "What time do you leave?"

"In about two hours. I'll have Elam fax you a copy of my itinerary."

Relieved they were on a more neutral topic, she nodded. Elam was probably just glad to get Trey out of her reach. A waiter took their orders, then they buttered miniature croissants.

"You gave me quite a scare last night," he said. "Are you sure you're feeling well?"

"Fine," she assured him. "And I'm signing up for swimming lessons next week. I'm sorry, Trey, I know the last couple of days have been somewhat of an embarrassment for you."

He shrugged. "You can't fault the guy's taste."

"You're being very gracious."

"I'm being very jealous."

Guilt stabbed her and she smiled to cover it. "There's no need."

"You're right." Trey shook his head, then raised his glass of juice. "As if you would be interested in a construction worker."

At his slightly condescending tone, a small part of her rallied in Ladden's defense. Twisting the napkin in her lap, she chose her words carefully. "He's a hardworking businessman, Trey."

"He runs a junk store."

"Antiques," she corrected quietly. "Ladden's Castle is a good resource for me. It's important to offer one-of-a-kind items to my clients."

"Like the mysterious rug you told me about?" he teased. "When am I going to see this magnificent carpet?" Lifting her hand, he kissed her fingers and murmured, "That hardwood floor isn't the only thing cold in my bedroom lately."

A warm flush bloomed in her cheeks. "I'll try to have the rug delivered by the time you return."

"A risky purchase, though, considering I might only be in the mansion another couple of months."

"You're going to win this election."

He grinned. "I take it I have your vote?"

"Absolutely." In fact, the only thing she was certain of these days was that Trey McDonald was the best man to lead the state. It hurt to think she might have cost him votes.

His expression suddenly turned serious. "Stick with me, Jasmine, and we'll go to the top. I need you. The public loves the idea of us being together. That's why this thing with Sanderson has gotten so much press."

She understood perfectly, because she also loved the idea of being with Trey. They made a great couple: youthful, successful, photogenic. They *looked* like they belonged together. What she felt had to be akin to what Jacqueline Bouvier felt when she met the young Jack Kennedy. A life with Trey McDonald would be filled with glamour, travel, money, and power. And love? Love took years, she told herself. He was a good man with a kind disposition—successful unions had been built on much less.

He snapped his fingers. "I don't know why I didn't think of it before. Go with me!"

She blinked in surprise. "On the campaign tour?"

"Sure—what better proof that all is well between us?"

"Well," she said, hesitating. "I hadn't planned on being away from my office for so long, but . . ."

"Great!" he said with a broad smile. "Let's hurry so you can go home and pack. I'll send a car for you."

"But what on earth will I do?"

"Just smile and court the press," he said, then

paused significantly. "I hope this will be the first of many road trips."

Jasmine smiled tremulously. "Right."

"Be careful what you wish for," she said to her reflection as she packed, "it might just come true."

Leaving with Trey was for the best, she'd decided during the drive back to her condo, although she couldn't quite put her finger on why spending the next several days with him and his entourage left her feeling so displaced. Scant hours ago she'd been contemplating spending a lifetime with him.

She finished packing in record time. After lugging her bags to the front hall, she performed a quick walk-through to check appliances and thermostats, then settled in an armchair in her living room to wait for the car. Her gaze kept roving to the copper lamp, one of the few bits of color in the otherwise stark room, made more vivid by a single red-winged butterfly that seemed determined to roost on the spout. With her limited knowledge of insects, she presumed the luster of the polished metal provided the attraction. Finally, unable to resist the pull herself, she rose and walked over to pick up the lamp.

The butterfly seemed content to remain, as long as she handled the piece carefully. Once again, she studied the Arabic symbols, surprised when more of the symbols clicked in her memory. Squinting at the etchings, she tried to translate the words. "Something, something, dwell, no, house . . . or home. Something, something, home. Maj . . . magenta . . . no, majesty. Majesty home?" Jasmine frowned. "Majesty's home? Not majesty . . . magic? Magician!" she squealed, causing the insect to take flight. "Magician's home!" Then she frowned again. "Magician's home?"

Ladden's words came back to her in a rush. *"This homeless guy says he lived in the copper lamp you bought and is going to grant me three wishes for releasing him from bondage."*

The air suddenly felt cool and she shuddered, hurriedly pushing the lamp onto the mantel. A magic lamp? Rubbing her bare arms briskly, she laughed. More likely the words of a clever souvenir salesman, she decided, then shrugged into her suit jacket and checked her watch. The driver was late. At this rate, she'd be sprinting through the terminal, if she made it at all.

Purposely turning her back on the copper lamp, Jasmine refused to let the nagging thoughts of Ladden Sanderson materialize. All his talk about genies and wishes and migratory rugs had seemed enchanting last night, but today it sounded just plain . . . well . . .

"Enchanting," she ruefully admitted, then massaged her temples with a groan.

The phone rang, startling her. She yanked up the handset, again checking her watch. "Hello?"

"Ms. Crowne?" asked a man's voice.

"Yes."

"My name is Jorrie—I'm supposed to deliver you to the airport." His tone was agitated.

"Is everything all right?"

"I'm on a cell phone. My limo stopped on the bypass."

She would miss the flight, but she could catch up with Trey later this evening or tomorrow. "I hope it isn't a serious repair," she offered, feeling sorry for the man who was probably worried about what the governor would say.

"I've been around cars all my life," Jorrie said, his voice shaking, "but this is the strangest thing I ever did see."

"What's wrong?" she asked, a finger of premonition tickling her spine.

"Butterflies . . . hundreds of 'em—maybe thousands—all over the engine, coming out from under the hood like colored smoke."

In her stunned silence, the driver apologized over and over. Jasmine mumbled something about putting in a good word for him with Governor McDonald, then hung up slowly. Had a strange butterfly pestilence descended on the city? In a daze, she called Trey's mobile phone to explain, but to her surprise, Joseph Elam answered.

"Joseph, this is Jasmine Crowne."

"Yes?" His voice sounded pinched.

"May I speak to the governor?"

"He's indisposed," he said without elaboration.

"The limo broke down on its way to pick me up. Tell Trey I'll have to catch a later flight."

After several seconds' pause, Elam asked, "Do you really think that would be wise, Ms. Crowne?"

"Excuse me?"

He sighed dramatically. "When the governor told me he had invited you along, I had my doubts about your presence on the tour."

A seed of anger took root in her stomach. "Could you be more specific?"

"The governor's political career hinges on the events of the next few days. He needs to be focused on the campaign, with no distractions."

"I want what's best for Governor McDonald, too," she reminded him.

"Then may I suggest that you stay in Sacramento, and stay out of trouble."

She pressed her lips together, then asked, "Anything else?"

"Actually, yes. You can give reporters a personal tour of the refurbished mansion, including the governor's personal quarters. I'll make the necessary phone calls to the media." He paused, as if in thought, but she prepared herself for a final dig. "Showing what you do for a living might help the public swallow the story about your *business* relationship with that Sanderson fellow."

"It's not a story," she said through clenched teeth.

"For the governor's sake," he said grimly, "I hope not."

Realizing that Elam was simply doing his job—watching out for the governor's best interests—she retreated gracefully. "Make those phone calls. I'll tie up the loose ends at the mansion and schedule the tours for tomorrow afternoon. Please inform the governor of your—I mean, *our* change of plans."

"Very good," he said. "Ms. Crowne, I hope you understand how important this election is to *all* of our futures."

Jasmine was silent a moment, then said, "I do, Mr. Elam. Believe me, I have dreams, too."

"Then you'd better perform magic for those cameras tomorrow."

"Jasmine," Ladden said happily, squeezing the phone. "How are you feeling today?"

"I'm fine," she said, although she didn't sound fine. "Ladden, I want to apologize for my behavior last night. I have no excuse for leading you on like that and Trey doesn't deserve the way I treated him."

His heart fell. It wasn't the conversation he'd hoped for, but he had begun to understand the delicate position in which they'd put themselves. He'd spent most of the afternoon trying to get through to McDonald and tell him to call the dogs off his family's tavern. His call had finally been passed to a fellow named Elam. A mistake had been made, the man informed Ladden. The tavern would be reopened within the hour. But, he added, did Mr. Sanderson understand that he was to keep his relationship with Jasmine Crowne on a professional level? Yes, Ladden conceded—professional.

"You're right, Jasmine," he said, his stomach churning. "Things were much simpler before we . . . before." He cleared his throat. "So from now on, it's strictly business."

"Good," she said, her voice flooded with relief. "Now then, do you have a price on the rug? I'm prepared to buy, and I need it first thing in the morning."

His life had been nothing but turmoil ever since he found that stupid rug. If Jasmine wanted to give the misbehaving carpet to Trey McDonald, she was welcome to it. He pursed his lips and made a split-second decision. "I'll make you a deal."

"What kind of deal?"

"If you can help me figure out a way to get it down, I'll sell it for what I paid for it."

"You're kidding," she gasped, then stopped. "Did you say 'get it down'?"

"You heard me."

"Where is it?"

"The last time I checked, it was on the ceiling."

Her laughter rolled over the phone line. "You're joking, of course."

Knowing she'd have to see it to believe it, he relented. "Of course I'm joking. But I want you to inspect it very carefully before you decide. When can you come by?"

At her silence, he knew she worried about being seen at his place.

"You could wear a disguise," he said, only half-joking.

She laughed. "I think I'll simply bring my assistant, April."

He hoped the woman wasn't faint-hearted. "Sounds safe. When?"

"It's four-thirty now, how about six?"

"Broad daylight, blinds up, doors unlocked—I'll see you then," he said, his heart already thumping in anticipation.

Since he'd had such a profitable day, he decided to close early and get a haircut. Afterward, he walked down to Tabby's, relieved to see they were back in full swing. His Cousin Joey and Uncle Ernie sat at the bar. He joined them and signaled Malone for a beer.

"The drink's on me, cuz," Joey said. "I can't thank you enough."

"Huh?"

"Ah, don't play dumb. After the health inspector closed us down, I was so mad, I didn't know what to do. Then a few minutes later, I got a call from the governor's office."

The beer tasted especially bitter as it slid down Ladden's closed throat. "What kind of call?"

"Some guy who said he'd checked into the inspection as a personal favor for you. Said the inspector had made several errors and it would be taken care of, pronto." He lifted his hand in a little wave. "And it was."

Ernie grunted. "Sounds like the governor's mighty appreciative of what you did for Ms. Crowne."

"Something like that," Ladden agreed.

"Maybe McDonald could help with your insurance claim."

"I have a feeling we've collected our last favor from Trey McDonald," Ladden said dryly. "I need to call Saul and see where the adjuster stands."

Ernie shook his head. "It don't look good, son, considering you nearly strangled your only witness today."

Just the thought of Gene made his head hurt.

"You must have a date," his aunt Silvie said as she walked up.

Ladden scowled. "What makes you say that?"

She pointed to his ears. "Haircut."

"Ahh," Ernie said, nodding. "Those are fine looking ears, aren't they, Joey?"

"Gorgeous," Joey agreed. "Going to see Jasmine for a little *private* mouth-to-mouth?" The men laughed uproariously.

"Very funny. You two should go on the road."

"You'd make beautiful kids, you and Jasmine," Silvie told him.

"Wait a minute," Ladden said, holding up his hands. "For the record, Jasmine Crowne and I were never dating and never will. Period."

They were quiet for a few seconds, exchanging glances. "What happened?" Silvie asked.

"She's dating the *governor*," he said in exasperation. "Isn't that self-explanatory?"

"But I already told my friends to start thinking about wedding gifts. Wouldn't you like one of those electric ice cream makers?"

He sighed. "Aren't you getting a little ahead of yourself, Aunt Sil?"

She wagged a finger at him. "I saw the way you two looked at each other."

"We're just friends," he growled.

"Whatever you say," she sang. "But it looked like magic to me."

Ladden downed the beer, then set the empty bottle on the bar. "Thanks for the brew, Joey."

"Don't leave," Ernie said when Ladden stood.

"He's got friends in high places now," Joey reminded Ernie with a jab.

Silvie gave him a knowing smile. "Say hello to Jasmine for me."

Ladden shook his head and made his getaway. The beer had gone to his head quickly on an empty stomach, and the events of the last few days still didn't make sense. In less than a week he and Jasmine had gone from acquaintances to nearly intimate, then back to acquaintances. Only now it was worse—now they would be awkward acquaintances.

Every time he replayed their encounter at the party, he changed the ending. In his favorite version, they made passionate love in the changing room and twice again on the way home, then Jasmine chose true love in Glenhayden over fame and fortune as the state's first lady, and they lived happily ever after.

In the second version, they didn't have sex, but Jasmine came to him later to admit she loved him instead of the governor. Then they made love on the spot, and lived happily ever after.

In the third version, they made passionate love twice in the changing room and once by the pool, and although Jasmine admitted she loved him, she simply couldn't pass up the life of a statesman's wife.

He frowned. Only in real life did they *not* have sex and *not* live happily ever after.

At the store he showered quickly in the cramped bathroom, then changed to clean jeans and a red T-shirt. On the way to unlock the front door, he checked the storeroom ceiling and found the rug still hovering there. Scratching his head, he once again tried to come up with some reasonable explanation. Was it possible that something in the ceiling pipework had attracted the static-charged carpet? Or that a friend or relative had schemed to hang the carpet as a practical joke? Perhaps with the tallest stepladder he owned, plus a hook on the end of the longest pole he could find, he might be able to pull it down.

Or maybe the ladies would have a better idea, he thought as he approached the front door. Hell, he'd shoot a harpoon up there if he had to. He simply wanted the thing out of his store and out of his life.

When he looked out the door, Jasmine was climbing out of her car, much like the day she'd come in after the earthquake. Had it been only three days ago? It felt like a lifetime. God, he wanted to get to know her better, to find out if she was as wonderful as he suspected. Lithe and leggy in a loose pantsuit and her hair pulled in a high ponytail with a wide silver clasp, she looked like the princess Gene had dubbed her.

Ladden smiled. He hadn't meant to hurt the old man, just scare him a little. Indeed, Gene hadn't been back to the store. He'd have to ask Jasmine if she'd seen him hanging around.

She stopped on the sidewalk, glanced at her watch, then scanned parked cars on both sides of the street. Looking for her assistant, he presumed. How ridiculous that they had to resort to a witness just to transact business after hours. He grabbed a broom, opened the door, and stepped out on the sidewalk, hoping to have a word with her before their chaperone arrived.

Wheeling toward the door, she shielded her eyes from the slanting rays of the late sun. The wind had picked up suddenly, and almost certainty they would see a storm before morning. The light fabric of her pantsuit whipped around her, molding to her slight curves. "Hi."

He kept both hands around the broom handle

and fought the urge to drag her into his arms for a very hot—and very public—kiss. "Hi, yourself."

"April isn't here yet," she explained, her voice unnaturally high.

After a few seconds of awkward silence, he said, "You look better than the last time I saw you."

At last she smiled. "So do you."

They stood staring at each other, and Ladden wondered if she would avoid him after today—after she'd obtained the only thing of his that she'd ever really wanted, he realized with sad clarity. Forget his heart, his soul, his body . . . the rug, a gift for her boyfriend's bedroom, was what she desired most.

The sun went behind a dark cloud and a stiff gust of wind blasted over them, staggering Jasmine. "Let's go inside," he shouted over the whistling noise. After glancing up and down the street again, she nodded and followed him into the store.

The bell clanged noisily when he pulled the door closed behind them. "Whew! Must be a storm blowing in from the coast."

Smoothing a hand over her hair, she nodded. "That wind feels weirdly familiar—like that blast that threw me off balance last night."

Ladden discarded his broom but crossed his arms to keep his hands occupied and off Jasmine. "Are you sure you weren't pushed?"

Her dark brow crinkled. "I'm certain."

"You were completely alone?"

"Absolutely. Why?"

He shook his head. "Gene came in the store today and said something about arranging for you to fall into the pool. I was afraid he had pushed you."

"No." She tilted her head, her green eyes dancing. "He's filling your head with more fairy tales."

"Um, actually, Jasmine, I think you should take a look at the rug before your assistant arrives."

"I don't know—"

"I'll stay right here," he added quickly.

"Well, the storm will probably delay her for a few minutes," she conceded.

At that moment, it darkened noticeably outside, as if the sun had simply dropped from the sky. Streetlights flickered, then glowed, and a driving rain began falling in great, slashing sheets.

"Where did this come from?" Ladden asked, peering out the windows. "I can't even see your car from here."

When a dull peal sounded, Jasmine extracted a phone from her purse and slid up the antenna. "Hello? . . . April, where are you?" Concern cluttered her face. "No, I can handle it, I'm just glad you're okay. . . . Don't worry, I won't drive in this mess. . . . I'll see you tomorrow." She punched a button, then returned the phone to her bag.

Ladden had pulled a dusty radio from beneath

the counter. With one eye on Jasmine, he searched for a weather report. "Is your assistant all right?"

"She hydroplaned off a shoulder, but she's fine, just a little shaken up."

"Good . . . good that she's fine, I mean."

Her smile was tremulous, and she didn't make eye contact. "I guess I'll just wait out the storm here, if you don't mind."

He guessed she was weighing the consequences of being discovered in his company, so he offered her a tidbit of comfort. "Even nosy reporters won't be out in this soup." When he heard the strains of an official-sounding report coming over the tinny built-in speaker, he turned up the volume.

". . . dangerously high winds and torrential rain, visibility of zero. Residents are advised to take cover away from windows. The rain is expected to continue until dawn. The following roads are closed due to flash flooding: Bayview, Avon, Candlelight Court, Stanton . . ."

"Did he say Candlelight Court?" she gasped.

"Maybe not for long," he soothed, sensing her rising panic. He could practically see the barrier she'd erected around herself.

"Right." She inhaled deeply, then smiled. "You wanted me to see the rug?"

"Let me grab a flashlight, just in case the electricity goes."

With the wind rattling the windows, he led the way back to the storeroom, wondering how she would react to the carpet, if she would even believe he'd had nothing to do with putting it up there.

"I don't quite know how to explain this," he said before opening the door, "so I'll just let you make up your own mind."

Pushing open the door, he allowed her to enter, then he followed. One step inside the room, he froze, his eyes bulging.

"Greetings, Master."

Grinning wide, Gene bowed, then swept his arm toward a small table that had been lavishly set for two, complete with glowing candles.

THIRTEEN

Jasmine seethed. Twinkling crystal and romantic candlelight in a storage room made for a beautifully clandestine dinner. Ladden had set her up! She wheeled, standing on tiptoe to voice her outrage. "This is the lowest, dirtiest, most underhanded, conniving trick I've ever seen!"

He inched backward, his hands raised. "Jasmine, I swear, I knew nothing about this."

But she advanced, poking her finger into his chest for emphasis. "I . . . don't . . . believe . . . you!"

Gesturing to the old man, he said, "Tell her!"

"It is true what my Master says," the old man proclaimed, inclining his turbaned head.

Incredulous, she looked back to Ladden. "And I'm supposed to believe him? A man who claims to live in a copper lamp and grant wishes?" She laughed in amazement. "You know what I think? I think you're both nuts, and I think I'm getting out of here."

She turned to go, but the door leading to the showroom slammed shut inches from her face, and when she tried the knob, it wouldn't budge. Frantically, she tried to remember if she had anything in her purse to use as a weapon. A cell phone, two lipsticks, and a fountain pen. Slowly, she turned until her shoulderblades scraped against the door. "I'm warning you two—I have a b-black belt in karate." An outrageous lie, but what did she have to lose?

"Jasmine, wait," Ladden said. "No one's going to hurt you." He walked purposely toward the old man. "You, on the other hand . . ."

The man's eyes widened until the coal black centers were framed in white. "Master, I arranged for you and your princess to be alone. The wind, the rain—it is all for you."

Ladden stopped and glanced back to her. "I think he's schizophrenic. The man's lost touch with reality and I've been letting him make *me* crazy."

"How can I convince you?" the man asked, splaying his hands and talking hurriedly in broken English. "You rub the magic lamp and release me from shackles of many centuries. I call you Master, say I will grant you three wishes." He shrugged, looking bewildered. "I grant the two wishes you made and sent you—how you say?—confirmation, yet you still don't believe in magic."

Smiling fondly in her direction, he continued. "I know my master loves the fair princess Jasmine, and although I cannot make her love him back, I can help."

Her cheeks warmed, and Ladden shifted nervously.

Gene pointed a bony finger at her. "I arrange blister on heel and for women's dressing room door to lock, so she will use men's."

A strange tingling started in Jasmine's fingers.

Then he pointed toward Ladden. "When you arrive, I arrange for door to lock behind you." The man sighed. "Still it was not enough, so I arrange wind to blow princess into water and for screams to reach your ears." He sighed louder. "Still no lovey-lovey." Scowling, he said. "Then Master choke me! Today I work hard—break down very long car of driver to—how you say, postpone?—trip with other man. Then I steer car of woman who works with you, arrange storm, and fix table."

Jasmine started to tremble. How could one crazy little man plan all this?

The man gestured wildly. "Still no lovey-lovey and still no believe in magic." Grabbing his turban with both hands, he wagged his head. "Americans have hard heads and hard hearts."

Jasmine inched forward until she stood slightly behind Ladden, shielded—from what, she wasn't sure—by his wide shoulders. "H-how do you know all these things?" she asked.

The man looked at her as if she were dense. "I am a genie."

"When you say 'arrange,'" Ladden said, "what do you mean?"

"Arrange?" The man's face wrinkled into a frown. "Make happen." He waved his arms, as if this movement would explain everything.

Jasmine cleared her throat. "You expect us to believe that you have magic powers?"

"It is not so strange," he said simply. "Centuries ago, there were many genies doing good things all over the world. But some began to do bad deeds, and their powers were taken away."

"Taken away by whom?" Ladden asked.

"The Genie Of Divine," he said matter-of-factly, lowering his voice in reverence as he glanced heavenward. Then he straightened and once again indicated the beautifully set table. "So you will eat and lovey-lovey?"

Ladden glanced over his shoulder and whispered, "What do you think?"

Slightly numb, she whispered back, "I'm a little fuzzy on the lovey-lovey part, but from the sound of that storm, we're going to be here for a while, and I'm hungry."

"We'll probably find peanut butter and jelly sandwiches under those silver trays," he murmured.

"Fine by me—I'll have a chance to inspect the rug." She nodded toward the carpet that lay stretched in the space cleared for the table—on the floor. "Just get rid of the old man."

Ladden's gaze bounced back and forth between the rug and the ceiling several times.

"What's wrong?" she whispered.

"Never mind," he said. "I'll get rid of him."

But when they turned back to Gene, he was gone.

"He's a kook," Ladden said, pivoting all around. "But he's a slippery kook."

"He certainly went to a lot of trouble," she said, surveying the table.

A beige lace tablecloth had been draped over a small Queen Anne table, its corners gathered and tied with large, pale yellow bows. More lace table-cloths tied with similar bows had turned mis-matched chairs into special creations. A complex table service for two had been created from many different antique china patterns and silverware, with domed silver lids covering the top plate. The crystal wineglasses and water glasses sparkled, re-flecting the flames dancing atop the elaborate sil-ver candelabra. A huge green vase held white and purple striped lilies, and a bottle of white wine chilled in a pewter bucket.

"Are all these things from your store?"

"Besides the flowers and the wine, yeah, al-though you'd never recognize them," he said, peeking under a tablecloth.

Jasmine lifted one of the domed lids. "Oh, my. This is not peanut butter and jelly."

Ladden craned his neck, his eyes widening. "Rack of lamb?"

"One of my favorites," she breathed.

"Mine, too," he said, lifting the other lid to find the same.

"And mushrooms!" she squealed.

He grinned at her, igniting desire low in her stomach. "We agree on two foods, it seems. Let's eat."

Ladden pulled out her chair, which made her a little nervous. When she'd planned her evening, sharing a romantic dinner with Ladden Sanderson had not been on the list. With his hair so neatly shorn, he looked boyishly handsome, a direct contradiction to his well-developed physique. The single most vivid impression she'd carried away from their encounter at the party was that she'd never felt so protected, so wanted, so cared for as she did standing in the circle of Ladden's arms.

"Wine?" he asked, uncorking the bottle.

She nodded and watched, mesmerized, as he filled her glass with the pale liquid. The dancing candlelight distorted the collection of furniture lining the walls, projecting immense images on the ceiling. The effect was slightly spooky and very intimate. "If someone walked in," she said softly, "this would be hard to explain."

Filling his own wineglass, he said, "I've given up trying to explain things lately." He raised his glass toward hers. "To magic."

But Jasmine stubbornly refused to believe the

fantastic things the little old man had described, despite his uncanny accuracy. Cautiously, she touched her glass to his. "Coincidence maybe."

After a deep sip of wine, he said, "Gene's right—you're a tough nut to crack."

Jasmine drew the sweet, cool liquid into her mouth and swallowed. "No, I just stopped believing in fairy tales a long time ago."

At her serious words, he met her gaze. Her body responded instantly to the desire in his eyes, remembering all too well the feel of his lips on hers. But above the nearly palpable physical attraction, she felt an odd connection with Ladden, an unconditional attachment so strong, it felt . . . ancient.

"Jasmine," he said quietly, "a few days ago, I would have agreed with you. But after this week—" He broke off, shaking his head. "For just a few hours, let's allow ourselves to believe that anything is possible."

Except it was dangerous to pretend—to be lulled into a soft, make-believe world where the harsh outline of reality was blurred. She knew that was true because here in the warm cocoon of their private dinner, living and loving the rest of her life with Ladden Sanderson not only seemed plausible, it seemed desirable.

"Okay," she whispered. "For just a few hours."

And as if they had indeed been thrust into a dimension where perceptions and expectations were abandoned, she allowed herself to be vulnerable to what Ladden had to offer. The sexual energy bounding between them unleashed itself in the room, enveloping them so completely, they might have been moving in slow motion. Suddenly, the simple act of eating seemed fraught with innuendo—every smooth slice and urgent bite of the delectable lamb, every savored swirl of the heady wine, every musky mouthful of the black mushrooms.

When Ladden deserted his half-eaten meal with a clatter of abandoned utensils and reached for her, Jasmine was hungry for him. Their mouths came together almost violently, their tongues battling, their lips devouring. He moaned her name, somehow expressing his need for her in mere guttural syllables. She wound her arms around his neck and pressed her breasts into the hard wall of his chest. He cupped her rear and effortlessly lifted her against his hard arousal, wrenching a gasp from her throat. Her limbs weakened and she allowed herself to be swept away on a wave of desire so strong she felt powerless to resist. Despite the warning bells chiming in her head, something else told her if she stopped now, her life would be somewhat less than it might have been.

As if he'd read her mind, Ladden lifted his head and touched her cheek with a trembling finger. His dark eyes glowed with passion. "Jasmine," he whispered, "if you want me to stop, please tell me now."

"No, don't stop," she murmured. "Please don't stop."

The room spun for a moment, then she felt the wool of the carpet at her back. Ladden lowered himself beside her, his breathing ragged and shallow. She pulled his mouth to hers, and their hands roamed over each other's bodies. Anxious to explore his expansive chest, Jasmine lifted the hem of his thin cotton shirt and helped him drag it over his head. Enthralled, she ran both hands over the alternately rounded and planed muscles of his chest and arms, tracing the outline of flat nipples indented in firm skin, squeezing his biceps. A triangle of black hair trailed down to disappear into his waistband. "Beautiful," she whispered.

He slid his hands under her loose blouse, caressing her stomach with his thumbs, then shimmying up her waist and fingering the sensitive skin of her rib cage. His broad, seeking fingers felt coarse and strong. The desire for him to touch every inch of her swelled and she tore at her clothing, their hurried movements magnified in shadows on the walls. When only her filmy white panties remained, she clambered up and astride him, savoring the texture of denim between her thighs and the look in his eyes as she arched above him, thrusting her bare breasts in the air. He reached up to unclasp her hair and as she rocked forward, grinding against him, her hair fell forward in a dark curtain, sweeping his chest. He groaned his approval and cupped her breasts, thumbing her dusky nipples until she cried out for him.

She slipped her fingers to his fly and unfastened the jeans, longing to see all of his magnificent body. He shifted and together they removed the rest of his clothes. His straining shaft glistened with his excitement, and she knew she was warm and wet.

"Jasmine, I want you," he rasped, rolling her beneath him and smoothing her hair away from her face. "I've always wanted you."

Quivering with her need for him, she stared into his passion-glazed eyes and said, "Ladden, at this moment, I'm yours."

They came together in another kiss, a promise of how wonderful their lovemaking would be. He slipped his hand inside her panties and she opened to his probing fingers. Latching on to a nipple, he drew the puckered skin into his warm mouth and nipped at the beaded tip while he made love to her with his hand. She writhed beneath him, thrusting to match the rhythm of his skillful fingers. When her moans began to escalate and she felt a burgeoning climax, he transferred his kisses to her neck and earlobe.

"Jasmine," he whispered. "Open your eyes, I want you to see my love for you."

Overwhelmed by the emotions flooding her, she struggled, but managed to open her eyes. His dark brow was furrowed with his concentration on pleasing her and he studied her face, poised to respond to the slightest movement. His eyes widened with hers as the first wave of climax descended.

"Oh, Ladden," she moaned, pulsing around his fingers, clawing at his shoulders as the orgasm mounted, crested, then slowly seeped away. "Ladden . . . oh, Ladden."

He nuzzled her jaw until she stilled, then slowly withdrew his hand. "Jasmine, I have to have you now," he said urgently.

"Now," she murmured, looping her arms around his neck.

"Are you protected?" he asked.

She nodded and his erection surged against her thigh in anticipation. Her desire for him was so great, she trembled. Slowly he settled between her legs, raining kisses over her face and breasts, then entered her in one slow thrust.

The storm outside renewed its force, crashing and booming around them, the wind barreling past the windows like a locomotive. Jasmine cried out with pleasure as their bodies melded, and Ladden choked out her name. He slipped his hands beneath her hips to angle their bodies perfectly for each long, powerful stroke. Within seconds, she felt another climax building, this one deeper, like a vibration at her very core. His eyes were open, his mouth alternately stretched in ecstasy and clenched with restraint. At the top of each thrust, she tightened around him and he moaned. Synchronized, they moved together, faster and faster until she yielded to another orgasm, and his shuddering release came before hers had subsided. "Jasmine . . . Jasmine . . . Jasmine."

As they lay together, unmoving, Jasmine clung to him and listened to the ferocious storm outside, her eyes already tearing in preparation for the inevitable storm inside.

"What's this?" he asked, lifting his head. He wiped at the corner of her eye with his finger, then he smiled. "I can't say I've ever moved a woman to tears before."

She inhaled deeply. "Ladden—"

"Shhh," he whispered. "Not yet. Let me hold you for a while."

He eased their bodies apart, then retrieved a quilt. Frightened by the extent of their wrongdoing, she slipped on her underwear while he rummaged for his boxers. But when he came back to the rug and reached for her hand, she went to him readily and they curled together. As if he could read her troubled thoughts, he caressed her arm slowly and continuously, and occasionally whispered, "It'll be all right."

Jasmine wasn't sure how long she'd slept, because when she opened her eyes, she was surrounded by blackness so thick, she couldn't even see her hand in front of her face. And it had turned cold—a window must have blown open because a breeze whipped over their bodies. Beneath the quilt, she snuggled closer to Ladden's heat, then sat straight up when she recognized the sound of an engine whine, growing louder and louder. Had an appliance been struck by lightning during the storm?

He was sleeping soundly, evidenced by his soft snores. Concerned, she swung her feet over the edge of the carpet, terrified and disoriented when her feet sank into freezing nothingness instead of the floor she expected. She jerked back, lying completely still as close to Ladden as she could without being on top of him. Her mind spun, and she forced herself to concentrate. Where was she? Had he carried her to another location inside the store?

The carpet seemed to be vibrating . . . almost as if they were moving. But that was ridiculous. Then, incredibly, she identified the distant lights overhead as . . . stars, and realized the open window was actually the outside air blowing around them. How romantic—Ladden had carried her to the roof while she slept. She smiled into the darkness and reached over to give his shoulder a shake.

"Hmmm?" he mumbled sleepily, pulling her closer. "What's wrong?"

"Why didn't you tell me we were outside?" she murmured into his ear. "I might have walked off a ledge or something."

"You're dreaming," he whispered. "Go back to sleep—or we could make love again."

She poked him again. "I'm not dreaming, and I

need to go to the bathroom. How do I get back inside?"

He shifted, wrapping his arm around her waist. "I don't mind that you talk in your sleep—it's a trade-off I can live with." He reached up to cup her breast.

"Ladden, I'm serious," she hissed. "Where's the light and where's the bathroom?"

He sighed and relinquished her breast. Her eyes had adjusted somewhat and she saw him push himself up to a seated position and stretch his arms in a wide yawn. Then he froze. "What the hell? Where are we?"

"Outside," she repeated patiently. "Don't you remember carrying me to the roof?"

"Jasmine, I don't have access to the roof. What is that noise?"

"It sounds like an engine or something. I thought maybe an appliance had been struck by lightning."

Whatever it was, it was approaching fast. The noise grew louder and louder. Terrified, Jasmine pressed her face into Ladden's chest. "What is it?" she cried as the roar became deafening and a massive object passed overhead, sending freezing blasts of air over them.

She could hear and feel his heart pounding in his chest. Slowly, the sound dissipated and at last she raised her head. "What was that?" she repeated. "And where are we?"

"Well," he said, his voice shaking slightly, "I'm

not positive, but I think it was an airplane . . . and I think we're, um, flying."

"Flying?"

"Look over there," he said, pointing.

Jasmine turned her head slowly and swallowed hard when she recognized the runway lights of the airport, far, far beneath them. "How is this possible?" she breathed.

"Again, I'm not positive, b-but it appears we are unsuspecting hitchhikers on a magic carpet ride."

"But that's insane!"

"Jasmine," he said, pointing again. "Isn't that the Arco Arena?"

"I'm not going to look," she shouted, hiding her face.

"Hey! There's the Air Force Base."

"This . . . is . . . not . . . happening."

"I'll bet we can see all the way to Lake Tahoe!"

"Ladden!" she yelled, on the verge of hysteria. "Listen to yourself."

"I can't explain it, Jasmine," he said in her ear, then he dropped a kiss on her neck. "But I do know a lot of weird things started happening when I bought this rug."

"Don't forget the lamp," she added.

"And the lamp. Look! There's my store!"

Moving in millimeters, she turned her head to peek just as they banked.

"Whoa," Ladden said, tightening his grip on her. "Now look."

She lifted her head and was rendered speechless.

They were wrapped in a quilt in their underwear, flying on the carpet high above Sacramento. The long fringe on the ends of the rug buffeted in the wind, and her hair blew around her head. It was a moonless sky, but millions of stars twinkled above them. The air around them had a bluish cast and smelled fresh. Beneath them, white and neon lights glowed, outlining the grid of the city. Now that the airplane had passed overhead, all was quiet, as if they were watching a silent panoramic movie. The scene was glorious, amazing, and utterly unbelievable.

Stupefied, she huddled next to Ladden and said, "Maybe there's something to this genie stuff, after all."

FOURTEEN

They landed with a thud.

Jasmine's eyes popped open and she sat straight up, clutching the quilt to her chest and gasping for breath. Diffused light from the alley filtered in the high windows above the rear entrance. The wind and rain still howled outside. Next to her, Ladden sprawled on the carpet, snoring softly. Remorse hit her so hard, she felt dizzy with nausea. Tears filled her eyes and spilled freely down her cheeks. She pushed her hair out of her face, her hand meeting a rat's nest of tangles. Gingerly, she pulled herself to her feet, her chest heaving with sobs, her hand over her mouth to muffle the hiccuping sounds.

She checked the time, her knees weak with relief to discover it was only nine-thirty. The gloominess of the storeroom and the general darkness of the storm had warped her perception of time . . . not to mention that incredibly vivid dream. Probably the mushrooms, she decided. Jasmine shook her head to clear her crazy thoughts and make room for the problem at hand—how to get out undetected.

But the enormity of the situation crushed her. What had she done? Sold her future—and possibly Trey's—for a few moments of pleasure with Ladden? Her hands shook uncontrollably as she pulled her blouse over her head. In the few seconds it took to find her slacks, she approached hysteria. At last she found the silk garment, entwined somehow with his jeans. She eased into them gingerly, already stiff and sore from their ardent lovemaking.

Jasmine snatched a linen napkin from the table to swipe at her eyes, but the very sight of their abandoned meal renewed her torrent of tears. Only one candle still burned, but it was fizzling out in its own wax, so she blew it out. The other half-burned candles must have extinguished themselves, she decided. Yet another careless mistake: they might have torched the entire block.

As quietly and quickly as possible, she repaired her hair and makeup with the limited contents of her purse. God only knew who might be lurking outside in their car with a camera at this very moment, waiting for her to emerge. She slung her purse to her shoulder and glanced back at Ladden, who still hadn't moved. She had a terrible feeling the worst was yet to come.

She took a deep breath and passed through the door to the fully lit showroom. If not for the rain,

she would have been perfectly spotlighted for anyone watching from outside, but she could barely
see her car across the street. Quickly, she unlocked
the front door, then stepped outside and made a
run for it.

A telephone rang in the distance, but by the
time Ladden roused, it stopped. He sat up and surveyed the room, knowing Jasmine was gone. At
least the rain had stopped. He sighed, passing a
hand over his face. Her leaving without waking
him was not a good sign.

But as he pushed himself to his feet, he could
not resist a little self-satisfied smile. What an incredible evening—first dinner, then their lovemaking, then the carpet ride. He laughed. Of course,
he could never repeat the story, but how appropriate that he had experienced the amazing event with
Jasmine. Glancing down at the rug, he said, "I was
beginning to think you had no redeeming quali-
ties."

The phone rang again and he reached for the
extension on his bookshelf.

"Hello?"

"Hi . . . it's Jasmine."

His heart vaulted at the sound of her voice.
"Where are you?"

"On my way home." She sounded curt, distant.

"Why didn't you wake me?"

In the instant of her hesitation, he knew he had

lost her. "I thought it would be best to simply leave."

Hurt pierced his heart. He closed his eyes and pressed his lips together, then said, "Can we discuss this?"

"My behavior was reprehensible," she said quickly, her tone cool. "I only hope all of us can get through this unscathed."

As always, she was worried about McDonald. "I'll do my part," he promised tightly.

"Thank you."

"I thought your road was closed by the flooding."

"I just heard on the radio that it's reopened." She cleared her throat politely. "Ladden, under the circumstances, I think it would be best if we don't see each other again—not even on a professional basis."

Another blow. "I see," he said. "And do I have any say in the matter?"

"No." Her voice was quiet.

"Well, then," he said with sarcastic cheer, "it's been good sleeping with you—have a nice life."

"Ladden, what happened was a mistake—"

"No," he cut in angrily. "The only thing wrong about it is that we're skulking around like teenagers."

"It was a one-night stand," she said flatly. "It meant nothing."

Her words cut him deeply, but he couldn't let them pass. "Tell yourself whatever is necessary to rationalize what happened between us, but I was there, and you can't tell *me* that it meant nothing." He took a deep, calming breath. "Look, I know all this magic stuff has got you spooked, but don't you see? How else could the two of us have gotten together?"

"Magic? I don't know what you're talking about," she said firmly.

Incredulity washed over him. "How can you say that after this evening—after the carpet ride?"

Silence stretched over the line. When she spoke, her voice shook. "Like I said, I don't know what you're talking about, but I really have to go. Good-bye, Ladden." And she hung up.

He stared at the phone, then slammed it down. His frustration and anger overflowed. Ladden strode across the room to the table where they'd eaten dinner and cleared the surface with one sweep of his arm. The horrific crash of glass and metal on the wood floor was only slightly therapeutic.

"Greetings, Master."

Ladden spun around to find Gene inspecting the mess. "Oh, it's you." He glanced at the floor sheepishly. I, um, got a little upset."

Gene sighed. "No lovey-lovey?"

Shifting nervously, Ladden wondered how much the genie had observed from whatever plane he lived on when he wasn't . . . visible. "Yes, there was lovey—yes."

"Then why this?" the man asked, gesturing to the heap of broken glass and flowers.

"It didn't make any difference. In fact, being together only made things worse. Jasmine doesn't want to see me anymore at all."

"Ah." The old man shook his head. "American women are stubborn, like a camel." Then he brightened. "You will find your princess someday."

Ladden pulled on his jeans, then nodded. "You're right. I can't make her love me. I need to get on with my life."

"Yes, and you still have a final wish." With a broad grin, he threw his arms wide. "What will it be?"

He laughed—he'd forgotten about the third wish. "Gee, I don't know—what do most people wish for?"

"Money . . . power." His eyes lit up. "I can make *you* governor, then you will have your Jasmine!"

Ladden frowned. "I don't want Jasmine to be with me because I have all the fancy trappings of some office. I'll leave that job to McDonald."

"Then how about gold?"

A definite possibility, Ladden thought wryly. But having the extra storefront would already provide him with the means to make a very comfortable living. "I can't decide. Do I have to use it right away?"

Gene shrugged. "No, but I must remain close until then."

"Let me have some time to think about it. I'm going home to get some sleep." When he turned around, Gene and the mess Ladden had made were gone. Whistling under his breath, he marveled at his own ability to adjust so quickly to having a genie around.

But on the drive home, Ladden set aside thoughts of genies and wishes and reflected only on the intimacies he and Jasmine had shared. The contours of her lithe body rose in his mind, amazing him all over again. Now that he'd had a glimpse of her sensual side, getting her out of his mind would be even more difficult.

And Jasmine hadn't heard the last of him yet. He was no genie, but he still had one trick up his sleeve.

"Ms. Crowne, a delivery van just arrived."

Jasmine glanced up at the secretary, her hands stilling on an onyx horse-head sculpture. "With the rug?"

"Yes."

She smiled in relief. A simple black woven rug was better than no rug at all. Jasmine stepped back to check the sculpture arrangement on Trey's dressing table. Satisfied, she joined the woman, checking her watch. "I only ordered it this morning. They said they could have it delivered by lunch, but this is even better."

"I told him to drive around to the west hall

exit. That way he won't have to carry it so far to the governor's room."

"Thank you, Ms. Rogers. I'll take it from here."

Jasmine smoothed a hand over her hair and checked her suit. She wanted to look her best when the cameras arrived, to show an outward appearance of calm, even if she were falling apart inside. Thankfully, she hadn't been followed home last night, and the news crews were too distracted by the freak storm to notice her car had been parked near Ladden's store for over three hours. If she were very, very lucky, maybe she and Ladden would be the only people who had to live with the knowledge of what they'd done.

When she walked into the west hall, she stopped abruptly. Her heart jumped to her throat at the sight of Ladden standing just inside the wide delivery door. He wore his usual jeans and T-shirt with a white ball cap that read Atlanta Braves. Every intimate act they'd shared last night flashed through her mind.

As she walked closer on rubbery legs, he removed his hat. "Hello," he said politely. No innuendo, no spite. Just hello.

"What are you doing here?"

His brow furrowed in puzzlement. "I brought your rug."

Alarm shot through her. She couldn't put that, that . . . *thing* in Trey's room and have it traveling the halls of the governor's mansion. "I changed my mind."

"But you said you had to have it," he said lightly. "You said it would be perfect for McDonald's room."

"I told you," she said, trying to keep her voice calm, "I changed my mind."

"From last night to this morning?" he asked, one eyebrow raised. "What happened to change your mind?"

What hadn't? "I decided it wasn't right for the room after all."

He shrugged. "Too bad. You asked for a rug, you've got a rug." Then he pulled out a pair of work gloves and turned toward the exit.

"But I don't want it!" she cried, trotting after him. With her luck, the rug would wait until the TV cameras were rolling, and then get up and do a jig.

When she walked out on the stoop, Ladden emerged from the truck with the rug resting on his big shoulder. "Which way is the governor's room?"

She didn't answer.

His mouth curved into a wry smile. "Don't tell me you've forgotten."

Pursing her lips, she sighed in resignation. Maybe she could get rid of it later. "Follow me."

Jasmine walked stiffly back to Trey's room, knowing Ladden perused her figure from only a few steps back. When she led him into the room, her skin tingled with the awkwardness of the situation.

Ladden lowered the rug gently to the polished wood floor. "Nice. My entire showroom would fit inside here."

She nodded, not knowing what to say.

He unrolled the carpet carefully and combed the fringe, touching the rug almost lovingly. "There. Your first instinct was right—the colors are great for this room." He turned a smile her way. "And how appropriate that this rug be in this room, don't you think?"

So she could remember their lapse every time she stepped into Trey's bedroom. Feeling light-headed, Jasmine reached for a chair to steady herself. "Ladden—"

"Jasmine, I love you."

Her chest felt ready to explode. Hot tears burned her eyelids, but she blinked them away and took a deep breath. "Ladden," she said quietly, "I'm not the right woman for you. We're very different people with very different goals in life."

He removed his hat, folding it in his hands. "I thought everyone wanted to grow old with someone they love."

"But I want . . . excitement and travel and fame." She measured her words, trying to be as honest with him as possible. She owed him that much. "Ladden, not very many people know that . . . that I came from absolutely nothing."

She swallowed and lifted her chin. "Being with Trey is the opportunity of a lifetime for me."

He didn't say anything for a while, just stared at her with sad, dark eyes. "So you're going to marry this man?"

She nodded curtly. "If he asks, then, yes, I'll marry him."

"And will he ask?"

"I think so, if he wins the election." She dropped her gaze.

"Well," he said slowly. "I guess there's only one thing I can do to make sure you're happy."

She glanced up, confused.

"I wish that Governor McDonald be re-elected."

Two seconds passed before the enormity of what he'd just done washed over her: he'd used his third wish. Her mouth opened, but no sound came out.

Ladden jammed his hat back on his head. "Good-bye, Jasmine."

FIFTEEN

Jasmine lay in her bed and watched as a bright blue butterfly walked the length of a still blade of her ceiling fan. Would she ever get them all out of her condo?

For two weeks, her life had resembled a whirlwind. The tours she'd given of the governor's mansion had made her friends in the media circles. Gradually, the rumors about her and Ladden had died while Trey McDonald had made the most amazing comeback in the state's political history. He'd won by a landslide, a surprise to everyone around him except her, she noted. The staff had celebrated for two days.

Today was the first day that she had no pressing appointments, no appearances with Trey, no congratulatory parties to attend. She dreaded it.

Because when her mind slowed for even a second or two, Ladden Sanderson was there, somewhere, loving her. With the entire unscheduled, unfrenzied, free-thinking day ahead of her, it would drag interminably.

After the election, she'd sent the magic carpet back to him along with a thank you note. No one else knew what he'd done for Trey—what he'd done for her. She hadn't heard back from him and didn't expect to.

Finally, she swung her feet to the floor and made herself get up. After a shower, she shuffled into the living room to have a cup of coffee and watch a local morning news program. Everyone, it seemed, was preparing for Thanksgiving dinner. She watched with mild interest as a local chef demonstrated how to clean the turkey and what to do with the giblets. An image of Ladden's family came to her mind, and she smiled. They probably had huge gatherings during the holidays.

Thanksgivings had stopped in her house when her mother died. As well as Christmases, birthdays, and any other reason to celebrate, as far as her father was concerned. He had never abused her physically, but he had tried to steal her heart, her drive, her ambition with his constant browbeating and too-strict rules.

Her heart swelled suddenly and she wondered if he'd changed in the fifteen or so years since she'd seen him. He still lived in the same little shack in Glenhayden. She drove by a couple of times a year just to make sure the name was still on the mailbox. Her most recent drive-by had been yesterday, and to her surprise, the house had been painted and the yard tidied. Her first sinking thought had been that he'd passed away and someone else was living there, but he'd been sitting in a lawn chair on the tiny porch, wiping his forehead.

He'd looked older and weaker, she thought, her heart hammering as she'd navigated her sportscar around the clunkers parked on the side of the street in the run-down neighborhood. She had almost stopped, but at the last minute she'd been much too frightened—her childhood had been an ugly, unhappy part of her life, and she didn't want it to taint her new life and her new image.

Her father wouldn't have a clue how to get in touch with her even if he wanted to—which had been the primary reason for changing her last name as soon as she became an adult. And even if he had purchased a TV or picked up a newspaper, he would never recognize her as the skinny little mouse she'd been under his thumb.

Still, the vision of him sitting alone in that lawn chair haunted her.

As she sipped her second cup of coffee, the program aired a feature segment on Trey and how the analysts were now saying that nothing would stop the man from reaching the White House. Her name was mentioned several times, and her face shown in conjunction with his. They played an excerpt from his acceptance speech and she was visible in the background, off to the right.

Halfway to her mouth, her hand stilled, sloshing a few drops of coffee. Everyone around her beamed, happy for the governor, thrilled for the party's victory. But the expression on her face . . . Did she always look that miserable?

Mesmerized, she watched herself wince as Trey mentioned her name in a long list of thank yous. And in that moment, she realized that Jasmine Crowne was a fraud. A fraud for traipsing around on the arm of a man she didn't love. A fraud for even considering marrying a man just to ride on his coattails into a life of celebrity. A fraud for pretending that family and goodness and true love didn't matter to her.

In fairness to Trey, she knew he was very fond of her, but he was looking for a marketing package for his future, and she fit the bill. He would be disappointed if she broke off their relationship, but he wouldn't be devastated. Neither one of them cared enough for that.

While she still had the nerve, she picked up the phone and dialed Trey's personal cell phone number. He answered on the second ring.

"Hello?"

"Trey, this is Jasmine. Do you love me?"

He laughed, obviously taken back. "Well, of course I do, dear," he said in his best campaign voice. "What kind of question is that?"

"I don't think you do, Trey, and that's all right because I don't love you, either."

Another laugh. "Listen, dear, would you like to meet for lunch?"

"Trey, I'm sorry that I haven't been truthful to you, but to be honest, I haven't been truthful to myself. I'm not cut out for a life in politics, and although I'm very fond of you, fondness isn't good enough for me, and I hope it isn't good enough for you."

"I . . . I don't know what to say—is it another man?"

"Yes."

"Is it Sanderson?"

"Yes."

He sighed. "So there is something going on between you two?"

"Actually, no."

"I'm confused."

"I told Ladden I wasn't interested. He's a gentleman, so he accepted my decision."

"I'm still confused."

"But I *am* interested, Trey. I just didn't realize it until now."

He sighed again. "Well, at least the election is over. The press is going to have a field day with this one."

"Trey, I haven't talked to Ladden. Nothing at all may come of this, but I wanted to clear the air before I told him how I feel, and to give you fair warning."

"Okay . . . thanks. I mean it, Jasmine, thank

you. I have the strangest feeling I wouldn't have won the election if it hadn't been for you."

She smiled into the phone. "Good-bye, Trey."

When she set down the handset, she felt as if an anchor had rolled off her chest. Taking a deep breath, she lifted the phone again and dialed directory assistance for Glenhayden. She copied down the number, then dialed again, her hands shaking.

The phone rang once . . . twice . . . three times. She started to hang up when a man's voice came over the line.

"Hello?"

She wet her lips and swallowed, summoning courage.

"Hello?" he repeated.

"D-Daddy? This is Jasmine."

Ladden adjusted the Help Wanted sign in the window. At least, he had decided on election day, he had the new storefront to keep his mind and body occupied. More space meant more furniture and antiques to gather, more refinishing, more repairs—he definitely needed to hire someone to help him, at least with the retail side.

And Saul had been so excited about the idea of doubled premiums, he had thrown his weight around to settle the insurance claim. Ladden stepped back to take a look around his new, expanded location. Things were going well, he had to admit, as far as business was concerned. But he hadn't made much progress in getting over Jasmine.

The bell on the door clanged and Ladden looked up to see an elderly gentleman in a suit walking toward him. "Hello, can I help you?"

The man inclined his head. "Greetings, Ladden."

Ladden's eyes widened. "Gene?"

The old man smiled, revealing his gapped teeth. "It is I."

"Where's the turban? And what's with using the door?"

"I'm trying to become more human. I think I might stay here in Sacramento, United States of America."

Ladden leaned on his counter. "What's her name?"

Gene grinned. "You're a smart one, you. Angelique—she is most beautiful artist."

"Does she know you're a genie?"

"No. That is why I get apartment, wear suit, and try to find job."

Ladden pursed his lips. "A job, did you say?"

"Do you know someone who needs worker?"

"Can you sell?"

Gene shrugged. "I can usually get humans to do what I want them to do."

"How much money are you asking for?"

The man scoffed. "Money? I not need money—I need job. Will work for free."

"You're hired," Ladden said, walking over to snatch the sign from the window.

"I cannot work now. I am having lunch with Angelique."

"Fine. Come back tomorrow morning. Oh, and Gene, I have the perfect housewarming gift for your apartment." He disappeared and came back carrying the rolled carpet.

"You do not want carpet?"

Ladden smiled wryly. "I think he needs to be with someone who truly understands his need to move around."

"Thank you!" Gene said in awe. "I cannot carry—I will fly carpet home to my apartment!"

Wincing, Ladden said, "Just try to be discreet, okay, Gene?"

"I'm sorry you haven't found princess."

Ladden waved off his concern, his heart twisting.

"I go now. Be back tomorrow." And he was gone, along with the carpet.

Looking around, Ladden shook his head. "So much for using the door."

The bell clanged again and he turned around, then stopped breathing. "Jasmine?"

"Hi," she said quietly.

She looked young and slim in loose jeans and a long-sleeved white blouse. Her thick plait hung over her shoulder. She was stunning, and he was so glad to see her, he couldn't speak.

"I, um, came to return this," she said with a nervous laugh.

For the first time, he noticed she was carrying the small copper lamp.

His heart dove, but he conjured up a polite smile. "No problem. Is something wrong with it?"

"Yes—it's defective," she said, sitting it on the counter, then walking toward him. She stopped within arm's reach, then stepped closer and slowly raised her arms around his neck. Dazed, he allowed her to pull his head down for a heart-stopping kiss.

"D-defective?" he asked, his mind spinning.

"Yes," she said, raining kisses all over his face. "I've been rubbing it . . . and rubbing it . . . and rubbing it . . . and my wish still hasn't come true."

His body reeled with love and desire as he pulled her close. "Is that so?"

Her lower lip came out in a pout and she nodded.

"Well," he growled in her ear, inhaling her scent and returning her kisses in kind, "what did you wish for?"

She pulled away to look into his eyes, and he felt humbled by the love so evident in her face. "For you to propose," she whispered.

His chest expanded with happiness. Beaming, he picked her up and whirled her around, whooping with joy. They were both laughing and dizzy when he finally set her down.

"Well," she prompted, "what do you say?"

Ladden yanked off his hat and immediately fell to one knee. Then he lifted her hand to his mouth and said, "Your wish is my command."

THE EDITORS' CORNER

For some, March can be one of the coldest months of the season. But those with a heartwarming LOVESWEPT in hand know that it's easy to stay cozy during the harsh winter. This month we're going to take you from peaceful Tylerville, Indiana, to wild Hell, Texas. You'll have a chance to hear the roar of a stadium crowd . . . the irritated grunts of an injured inventor. LOVESWEPT once again covers the spectrum of readers' tastes with this month's batch of romance!

Mary Kay McComas returns with **MS. MILLER AND THE MIDAS MAN,** LOVESWEPT #874. Every time Augusta Miller looks out her kitchen window she sees a huge Rottweiler sitting on her garbage-strewn lawn. Next door, Scotty Hammond smiles each time the same sixteen cans come sailing back over his fence. His plan to meet his new neighbor is a bit unconventional, but Scotty is known all over town for getting things done one way or another. Now he's set his sights on Gus, and she's having no part of it! Can the single dad next door convince the lovely violinist to be his partner in life's duet? Mary Kay is at her best in this hilarious, yet touching story about kindred spirits who have much to learn about love.

Neither Annie Marsden, R.N., nor Link Sheffield, Ph.D., have a high regard for the opposite sex. To Annie, men are competitive macho studs; to Link, women are flighty and irresponsible. Now both are fated to **CHASE THE DREAM,** in LOVESWEPT #875 by Maris Soule. Injured in a lab explosion, a grouchy Link must wait out his recovery before he can get back to his work. Annie has taken care of rude patients before, and the pay for this job as Link's live-in nurse can't be beat. But when new dangers force them into hiding, Annie's job description is drastically altered. Can Annie keep the wary genius safe from the shadows that threaten both their lives? Maris Soule revels in the ultimate mystery of love in this tale of combustible passion and romance on the run.

How far would you be willing to go for a pair of tickets to the hottest game of the season? Domenic Corso and Lynne Stanford are willing to go **THE WHOLE NINE YARDS,** in LOVESWEPT #876 by newcomer Donna Valentino. As die-hard Steelers fans, Dom and Lynne realize their last, best hope of obtaining playoff tickets is to enter the special lottery and apply for a marriage license. The pair had hoped to keep their sweetheart deal a secret, until word of their pending, albeit pretend, nuptials reaches their friends and family! Will this harebrained scheme win them the tickets to the game, or will it succeed in sending them down the aisle for real? Please welcome Donna Valentino as she shows us what happens when a game of let's pretend gives way to something more real than ever imagined!

Hell, Texas. Population 892, that's including the barnyard animals. In Eve Gaddy's **AMAZING GRACE**, LOVESWEPT #877, Max Ridell learns that Hell really does exist. Although after being thrown in jail for defending himself against the town bully, Max is beginning to wish he'd never heard of the one-horse town and its sheriff, Grace O'Malley. Gracie admits that she's not one to stick out in a crowd, but Max makes her want, just once, to be the kind of woman a man could really fall for. Max has a few secrets to hide and Gracie's determined to find out just what's going on in her jurisdiction. Eve Gaddy's tantalizing novel delivers an undercover lawman into the arms of a tenderhearted sheriff and makes for a showdown not to be missed!

Happy reading!

With warmest wishes,

Susann Brailey   *Joy Abella*

Susann Brailey   Joy Abella

Senior Editor   Administrative Editor

P.S. Watch for these Bantam women's fiction titles coming in February! *New York Times* bestselling author Amanda Quick once again stuns the world with

AFFAIR, now available in paperback. Private investigator Charlotte Arkendale doesn't know what to make of Baxter St. Ives, her new man-of-affairs. He claims to be a respectable gentleman, but something in his eyes proclaims otherwise. In **THE RESCUE,** by the versatile Suzanne Robinson, Primrose Adams disappears after witnessing a brutal murder on the streets of Victorian London. But when Sir Luke Hawthorne finds her, Primrose's secret pulls them together in a way neither can imagine. Hailed by *Romantic Times* as an author who "breathes life into an era long since past," Juliana Garnett returns with **THE VOW,** a dazzling medieval tale of intrigue and conquest. When William of Normandy sends his most trusted knight, Luc Louvat, to the northern reaches of Saxon England, Luc finds that it may be a lot more difficult to break down the defenses of a fair maiden than the fortress walls that surround her. And immediately following this page, preview the Bantam women's fiction titles on sale in January!

For current information on Bantam's women's fiction, visit our new Web site, *Isn't It Romantic*, at the following address:

http://www.bdd.com/romance

Don't miss these exciting novels
by your favorite Bantam authors!

On sale in January:

AND THEN YOU DIE . . .
by Iris Johansen

THE EMERALD SWAN
by Jane Feather

A ROSE IN WINTER
by Shana Abé

AND THEN YOU DIE . . .

by *New York Times* bestselling author Iris Johansen

Bess Grady is a hardworking photojournalist on an easy assignment. But what awaits her in a small-town paradise isn't pleasure; it's paralyzing fear. The unimaginable has happened in Tenajo—and Bess and her sister Emily have stumbled right into the middle of it. Suddenly, Emily disappears, Bess is taken captive, and escape seems impossible. But when rescue comes from an unexpected source, Bess is unprepared for the chilling truth. Tenajo was a testing ground—the first stage in a twisted game plan designed to spead terror and destruction. Now, to stop the ruthless conspirators whose next target may be the heartland of the United States, Bess must join forces with the intimidating stranger who led her out of Tenajo, a man whose motives are suspect, whose alliances are unclear, and whose methods have a way of leaving bodies in his wake. For she will do anything—risk everything—to save her sister, her family, and untold thousands of innocent lives.

"You slept well," Emily told Bess. "You look more rested."

"I'll be even more rested by the time we leave here." She met Emily's gaze. "I'm fine. So back off."

Emily smiled. "Eat your breakfast. Rico is already packing up the jeep."

"I'll go help him."

"It's going to be all right, isn't it? We're going to have a good time here."

"If you can keep yourself from—" Oh, what the hell. She wouldn't let this time be spoiled. "You bet. We're going to have a great time."

"And you're glad I came," Emily prompted.

"I'm glad you came."

Emily winked. "Gotcha."

Bess was still smiling as she reached the jeep.

"Ah, you're happy. You slept well?" Rico asked.

She nodded as she stowed her canvas camera case in the jeep. Her gaze went to the hills. "How long has it been since you've been in Tenajo?"

"Almost two years."

"That's a long time. Is your family still there?"

"Just my mother."

"Don't you miss her?"

"I talk to her on the phone every week." He frowned. "My brother and I are doing very well. We could give her a fine apartment in the city, but she would not come. She says it would not be home to her."

She had clearly struck a sore spot. "Evidently someone thinks Tenajo is a wonderful place or Condé Nast wouldn't have sent me."

"Maybe for those who don't have to live there. What does my mother have? Nothing. Not even a washing machine. The people live as they did fifty years ago." He violently slung the last bag into the jeep. "It is the priest's fault. Father Juan has convinced her the city is full of wickedness and greed and she should stay in Tenajo. Stupid old man. There's nothing wrong with having a few comforts."

He was hurting, Bess realized, and she didn't know what to say.

"Maybe I can persuade my mother to come back with me," Rico added.

"I hope so." The words sounded lame even to her. Great, Bess. She searched for some other way to help. "Would you like me to take her photograph? Maybe the two of you together?"

His face lit up. "That would be good. I've only a snapshot my brother took four years ago." He paused. "Maybe you could tell her how well I'm doing in Mexico City. How all the clients ask just for me?" He hurried on, "It would not be a lie. I'm very much in demand."

Her lips twitched. "I'm sure you are." She got into the jeep. "Particularly among the ladies."

He smiled boyishly. "Yes, the ladies are very kind to me. But it would be wiser not to mention that to my mother. She would not understand."

"I'll try to remember," she said solemnly.

"Ready?" Emily had walked to the jeep, and was now handing Rico the box containing the cooking implements. "Let's go. With any luck we'll be in Tenajo by two and I'll be swinging in a hammock by four. I can't wait. I'm sure it's paradise on earth."

Tenajo was not paradise.

It was just a town baking in the afternoon sun. From the hilltop overlooking the town Bess could see a picturesque fountain in the center of the wide cobblestone plaza bordered on three sides by adobe buildings. At the far end of the plaza was a small church.

"Pretty, isn't it?" Emily stood up in the jeep. "Where's the local inn, Rico?"

He pointed at a street off the main thoroughfare. "It's very small but clean."

Emily sighed blissfully. "My hammock is almost in view, Bess."

"I doubt if you could nap with all that caterwauling," Bess said dryly. "You didn't mention the coyotes, Rico. I don't think that—" She stiffened. Oh, God, no. Not coyotes.

Dogs.

She had heard that sound before.

Those were dogs howling. Dozens of dogs. And their mournful, wailing sound was coming from the streets below her.

Bess started to shake.

"What is it?" Emily asked. "What's wrong?"

"Nothing." It couldn't be. It was her imagination. How many times had she awakened in the middle of the night to the howling of those phantom dogs?

"Don't tell me nothing. Are you sick?" Emily demanded.

It wasn't her imagination.

"Danzar." She moistened her lips. "It's crazy but— We have to hurry. *Hurry*, Rico."

Rico stomped on the accelerator, and the jeep careened down the road toward the village.

They didn't see the first body until they were inside the town.

Let Jane Feather capture your heart once again with
the third and final book in her spectacular
"Charm Bracelet Trilogy"

THE EMERALD SWAN

by Jane Feather

Miranda, a gibbering Chip clinging to her neck,
dived into a narrow gap between two houses. It was so
small a space that, even as slight as she was, she had to
stand sideways, pressed between the two walls, barely
able to breathe. Judging by the cesspit stench, the
space was used as a dump for household garbage and
human waste and she found it easier to hold her
breath anyway.

Chip babbled in soft distress, his scrawny little
arms around her neck, his small body shivering with
fear. She stroked his head and neck even while silently
cursing his passion for small shiny objects. He hadn't
intended to steal the woman's comb, but no one had
given her a chance to explain. Chip, fascinated by the
silver glinting in the sunlight, had settled on the
woman's shoulder, sending her into a paroxysm of
panic. He'd tried to reassure her with his interested
chatter as he'd attempted to withdraw the comb from
her elaborate coiffure. He'd only wanted to examine
it more closely, but how to tell that to a hysterical
burgher's wife with prehensile fingers picking
through her hair as if searching for lice?

Miranda had rushed forward to take the monkey

away and immediately the excitable crowd had decided that she and the animal were in cahoots. Miranda, from a working lifetime's familiarity with the various moods of a crowd, had judged discretion to be the better part of valor in this case and had fled, letting loose the entire pack upon her heels.

The baying pack now hurtled in full cry past her hiding place. Chip shivered more violently and babbled his fear softly into her ear. "Shhh." She held him more tightly, waiting until the thudding feet had faded into the distance before sliding out of the narrow space.

"I doubt they'll give up so easily."

She looked up with a start of alarm and saw the gentleman from the quay walking toward her, his scarlet silk cloak billowing behind him. She hadn't paid much attention to his appearance earlier, having merely absorbed the richness of garments that marked him as a nobleman. Now she examined him with rather more care. The silver doublet, black and gold velvet britches, gold stockings and silk cloak indicated a gentleman of considerable substance, as did the rings on his fingers and the silver buckles on his shoes. He wore his black hair curled and cut close to his head and his face was unfashionably clean shaven.

Lazy brown eyes beneath hooded lids regarded her with a glint of amusement and he was smiling slightly, but Miranda couldn't decide whether he was smiling *at* her or *with* her. However, the smile allowed her to see that his mouth was wide and his teeth exceptionally strong and white.

Her own smile was somewhat uncertain. "We didn't steal anything, milord."

"No?" A slender arched black eyebrow lifted.

"No," she stated, flushing. "I am not a thief and

neither is Chip. He's just attracted to things that glitter and he doesn't see why he shouldn't take a closer look."

"Ah." Gareth nodded his understanding. "And I suppose some poor soul objected to the close examination of a monkey?"

Miranda grinned. "Yes, stupid woman. She screamed as if she was being boiled in oil. And the wretched comb was only paste anyway."

"That creature was on her head?" he asked, filled with compassion for the unknown hysteric.

"He's not a creature," Miranda protested. "He's perfectly clean and very good-natured. He wasn't going to hurt her."

"Perhaps the object of his attention didn't know that." The glint of amusement in his lazy regard grew brighter.

"That's always possible," Miranda conceded. "But I was about to take him away and they set on me, so what could I do but run?"

"Quite," he agreed, then cocked his head with a frown at the renewed sounds of a mob in full cry. "But I'm afraid they've realized you gave them the slip."

"Oh, lord of grace," Miranda muttered. "Come on, Chip." She turned to flee but the nobleman reached out and grabbed her arm.

"I have a better idea."

"What?" Miranda looked anxiously over her shoulder toward the sounds of the returning hue and cry.

"You'll be safer if you get off the streets for a while. That orange gown is as distinctive as a beacon. Come with me." He turned back toward the Adam and Eve without waiting for her assent and after an instant's hesitation Miranda followed him, Chip still clinging to her neck.

"Why would you bother with me, milord?" She skipped up beside him, her eyes curious as she looked up at him.

Gareth stared at her. The idea was far from fully formed, but the possibilities beckoned. "Would you be interested in a proposition?"

She looked up at him, and her blue eyes were wary. But she could see nothing in his countenance to alarm her. His brown eyes regarded her calmly, his mouth was relaxed. "A proposition? What kind of a proposition?"

A deeply enthralling, richly romantic novel of
passion and adventure by a stunning new voice in
historical romance . . .

A ROSE IN WINTER
by Shana Abé

*At sixteen, Lady Solange had pledged her love to Damon
Wolf, had dreamed they would be together forever. But
when her ruthless father threatened Damon's life unless
she agreed to marry another, Solange did the only thing
she could: she scorned her true love and sent him
away . . . never imagining the fate that awaited her,
never knowing that one day her destiny would be entwined
with Damon's once more.*

*For nine long years, Solange has lived a nightmare,
wed to a wealthy lord whose handsome face hides a soul of
darkest evil. Yet now, just as she is poised to finally make
good her escape, Damon suddenly appears at the castle
gate. Gone is the gentle hero of her childhood, replaced by a
fiercely attractive, thunderously angry knight, who makes
it clear he has never forgiven her betrayal. Convincing
Damon to escort her to safety will take all Solange's inge-
nuity—but the real challenge lies in breaching the walls
that Damon has built between them, to win back his
trust . . . and his hardened heart.*

> Solange.
> At last. It was a moment of epiphany. Here she
> was in front of him, a grown woman, a widow by her
> account. His mind was having a difficult time taking it
> all in.

But his body was not, by heaven. He wanted her as fiercely as he ever did. He nearly could not breathe for the want.

He would not crumble, no matter the cost. He wanted to shout at her, he wanted to know why she had rejected him, why she had rejected her father, her homeland. Instead, he kept his lips tightly shut, marking her reaction to his news.

She turned away from him, took a few blind steps to the thronelike chair topping the dais. She did not sit, however, merely stood next to it, arms crossed over her chest. He saw the shiver take her again and again. Her head dipped low.

"My lady," he began.

"My father is dead. The earl is dead. I find—" Her voice broke, a tremulous waver before she recovered. "I find that I cannot think right now. I must rest."

As if on cue, the court women swarmed over to her, taking her arms and leading her down the steps. In frustration, Damon watched them go. He felt robbed of his moment after coming all this way. It couldn't be over this quickly. He would not allow her to disappear just yet.

"Countess," he called.

Solange stopped, then turned. The women fanned around her.

"I am weary," Damon said clearly. "I have traveled far to reach you. I require food and a place to bed for the night."

His words seemed to snap at her, drawing her spine straighter. "Of course. Forgive my poor manners. I'll have one of the men show you to your chambers and arrange to have dinner brought to you. I'm afraid it is past the evening meal, but there is always plenty of food in the buttery."

She murmured instructions to one of the ladies, who curtsied and fluttered away.

"Someone will be with you shortly," she said. "Good eve to you."

They left as a group out the chamber door, a flash of gold in a wash of pastels.

The fire popped and sizzled behind an iron grate, echoing off the emptiness around him.

He was awakened from a sound sleep by a hand placed over his mouth.

In an instant he had drawn the stiletto from beneath the pillow and pressed it against the throat of his attacker. It was a move so deeply ingrained from the years of battle that it took him a full minute to realize that both the hand and the throat belonged to a woman.

To Solange, to be exact.

The dimming fire allowed just enough of the delicacy of her features to stand out in the darkness. She showed no reaction to the sharp dagger but looked down at him calmly, waiting for the recognition to sink in.

He drew the knife back, then pushed her hand away. "Are you mad?"

"Shh. You must speak quietly, lest they hear you."

He tossed the covers off himself and climbed out of the bed. He was almost fully dressed, another habit learned from battle.

"What is the meaning of this, Countess? You have no place here."

"Please, Damon, lower your voice. They must not find us!"

He stared at her in the darkness, baffled. Her urgency was real enough; he reckoned if the newly widowed countess was discovered with another man on the very night of the death of her husband, her reputation would not survive.

The Solange he knew wouldn't have given a shrug of her shoulders over something like her reputation, Yet, she was the countess now.

"Leave," he ordered curtly.

She approached him slowly, hands held out in appeal. "It is my every intention to leave. That is why I'm here."

"What?"

"I want to go with you back to England. I want us to leave here tonight."

He laughed softly. "Your wits are addled, Solange. Go back to your women."

She made an exasperated sound. "The hounds of hell could not drag me back there. I have to go with you, tonight, right now."

She looked so thin and lovely, and very serious. A heavy black cloak swirled around her ankles, but as she moved toward him he saw to his amazement that she was wearing a tunic, hosiery, and buckskin boots: men's clothing. She was still talking.

"We need to leave as soon as you may be ready. I'll help you if you like." In the darkness she took on the earnestness of a young girl, breathless and beguiling. "I can pack very quickly."

He shook his head. "You'll not go anywhere with me, Countess. I'm not courting that kind of trouble. Seek your adventures elsewhere."

She paused, looking as if his barb might have actually hurt. He ignored the flash of guilt. She would not use him, damn her, for whatever game she was playing. He would not submit to that.

"You don't understand." Her voice was subdued. "I have to go."

"And why is that?"

She chewed on her lower lip, another girlish habit he found suddenly annoying. But then her face cleared, became resolute. "If you will not help me, then I will go alone." The cape billowed to life as she swept past him toward an opening in the far wall he had not noticed before.

He caught her before she could vanish into the blackness.

"What is this, madam? You have deliberately put me in a room with hidden doors and secret tunnels? Is it so that you may creep in here in the disguise of nightfall? Is that your amusement these days, Solange?"

"Of course. I knew you would bolt your door closed tonight. How else was I to get in?"

Her look was so innocent, he practically could believe in her virtue again. Amazing, this acting ability she had discovered.

How convenient for her to have a room to keep her lovers nearby, tucked away from prying eyes. What sort of husband had Redmond turned out to be, to allow his wife this unusual freedom in his own home? Damon was almost sorry he could not question him for himself.

"But the man is dead," he muttered. Very interesting.

"Pardon?"

"Your husband. I have just remembered myself. You are a widow driven mad with mourning, no doubt. Someone should be watching over you."

She shook him off with supple strength. "You have changed greatly, Marquess. You should not be surprised to learn that I have changed as well. You speak now of things you could not possibly know anything about. My apologies. I didn't mean to disturb you."

Before he could think to respond, she was gone, her footsteps fading away down the tunnel.

"Damn. Damn, damn, damn."

It was no accident, he knew, that she had chosen to throw back at him his own words from their parting those years past. She was too clever for it to be anything else.

She wasn't really fleeing the estate. She wouldn't act so rashly, he reassured himself. She had nowhere to go that he knew of. It would be a folly beyond belief to think she could make it back to England on her own—a woman, a gentlewoman, who really knew nothing of the ways of the world. She could not be that foolish.

With a muttered oath Damon picked up his scabbard and secured it around his waist. It took only a few minutes to toss his scant belongings back into the traveling sack, but he could feel each second slipping by.

He hurriedly shoved his boots on and laced up the sides. She would be at the stables by now, or who knew where that tunnel let her out of the house. She might have already had a horse waiting in some hidden location, in which case he would have to track her either by sound or wait until dawn, when he could see her horse's prints.

By dawn the entire household would realize their mistress was missing. And who would they first suspect in this dangerous mystery?

On sale in February:

AFFAIR
by Amanda Quick

YOU ONLY LOVE TWICE
by Elizabeth Thornton

THE RESCUE
by Suzanne Robinson

THE VOW
by Juliana Garnett